From *Great Black Kanba*

He came along with me, holding my arm, and at the door he stopped me. "No—that wouldn't be proud enough." He bent down and, putting his arm around me, gave me a very fine kiss—the best, he explained immediately afterward, that Sale could offer.

"And very satisfactory," I conceded. "But aren't there any other boys in Sale?"

"I'll do it again sometime," he promised, with a glint in his eye, "and show you— Listen, get a move on, will you? I don't want this rendezvous to be a threesome."

"All right," I said, offended. "Have a good time. Mavis is just your type, and she'll fit perfectly into the Junior Matrons' Sewing Circle of Sale."

This struck me as being pretty funny, and I laughed all the way along the corridor of the next car. Mavis, with her bottle-washed hair, her couple of feet or so of eyelashes, and her lips painted on to suit Mavis and ignoring entirely the mouth God gave her.

When I reached my own car I found that everything was quiet. There was no sound from Uncle Joe's room, and I assumed that he must have recovered. The train flowed on, quietly and smoothly, and I remembered that the plain over which we were traveling was supposed at one time to have been completely under water. It felt, somehow, as though we were under water now.

Something moved on the floor, and I looked down just as a small lizard glided across and down the corridor. I caught my breath and stepped back, and the thing disappeared into the shadows at the end of the car.

I stood there, breathing fast and terrified that the creature would come back—and then I noticed that it had left tracks where it had crossed the corridor. I stooped over and looked curiously, and saw that the tracks were made with blood.

Books by Constance & Gwenyth Little

The Grey Mist Murders (1938)
The Black Headed Pins (1938)
The Black Gloves (1939)
Black Corridors (1940)
The Black Paw (1941)
The Black Shrouds (1941)
The Black Thumb (1942)
The Black Rustle (1943)
The Black Honeymoon (1944)
Great Black Kanba (1944)
The Black Eye (1945)
The Black Stocking (1946)
The Black Goatee (1947)
The Black Coat (1948)
The Black Piano (1948)
The Black Smith (1950)
The Black House (1950)
The Blackout (1951)
The Black Dream (1952)
The Black Curl (1953)
The Black Iris (1953)

Great Black Kanba

By Constance & Gwenyth Little

The Rue Morgue Press
Boulder, Colorado
1998

The Rue Morgue Press
P.O. Box 4119
Boulder, CO 80306

PRINTED IN THE UNITED STATES OF AMERICA

Great Black Kanba

About the Littles

Although all but one of their books had "black" in the title, the 21 mysteries of Constance (1899-1980) and Gwenyth (1903-1985) Little were far from somber affairs. The two Australian-born sisters from East Orange, New Jersey, were far more interested in coaxing chuckles than in inducing chills from their readers.

Indeed, after their first book, *The Grey Mist Murders*, appeared in 1938, Constance rebuked an interviewer for suggesting that their murders weren't realistic by saying, "Our murderers strangle. We have no sliced-up corpses in our books." However, as the books mounted, the Littles did go in for all sorts of gruesome murder methods—"horrible," was the way their own mother described them—which included the occasional sliced-up corpse.

But the murders were always off stage and tempered by comic scenes in which bodies and other objects, including swimming pools, were constantly disappearing and reappearing. The action took place in large old mansions, boarding houses, hospitals, hotels, or on trains or ocean liners, anywhere the Littles could gather together a large cast of eccentric characters, many of whom seemed to have escaped from a Kaufman play or a Capra movie. The typical Little heroine—each book was a stand-alone—often fell under suspicion herself and turned detective to keep the police from slapping the cuffs on. Whether she was a working woman or a spoiled little rich brat, she always spoke her mind, kept her sense of humor, and got her man, both murderer and husband. But if marriage was in the offing, it was always on her terms and the vows were taken with more than a touch of cynicism. Love was grand, but it was even grander if the husband could either pitch in with the cooking and cleaning or was wealthy enough to hire household help.

The Littles wrote all their books in bed—"Chairs give one back-aches," Gwenyth complained—with Constance providing detailed plot outlines while Gwenyth did the final drafts. Over the years that pattern changed somewhat but Constance always insisted that Gwen "not mess up my clues." Those clues were everywhere and the Littles made sure there were no loose ends. Seemingly irrelevant events were revealed to be of major significance in the final summation.

The Littles published their two final novels, *The Black Curl* and *The Black Iris*, in 1953, and if they missed writing after that, they were at least able to devote more time to their real passion—traveling. The two made at least three trips around the world at a time when that would have been a major expedition. For more information on the Littles and their books, see the introductions by Tom & Enid Schantz to The Rue Morgue Press editions of *The Black Gloves* and *The Black Honeymoon*.

Chapter One
WHO AM I?

THE FIRST TIME I opened my eyes, it was to a confusion of telegraph poles, wires, and treetops streaming past the square, dusty window, and I closed them and turned my head on the pillow, because it made me dizzy. I tried again, and this time the scenery was more or less stationary. A woman sat beside me, wedged in between my bed and a washbasin that was folded into the wall. She was a large woman, and she appeared to be sleeping with her mouth open. She was tied up firmly in a heavy purple dressing-robe, and two iron-gray braids dangled against her shoulders. Or were they plaits? I closed my eyes, feeling confused and faintly frightened.

I waited for a minute or two and then looked again. The woman was still there, but she was awake now and beaming at me.

"Feeling better?" she asked brightly.

"I feel all right." I raised my shoulders from the pillow, but I was dizzy and my head ached, so I eased back again.

"That's right. You just lie quiet there for a bit. We won't be in at Albury for another hour yet, and I'll give you a hand when the time comes. Here, try a drink of water."

She raised an arm to a glass carafe that was niched into the wall and poured bluish water into a tumbler, while her body braced itself clumsily against the motion of the train. I drank some water, but it had a flat, stale taste.

"You're pretty lucky, you know," the woman observed, shaking her head. "Your friend—the girl who was in here with you—she a relative or anything?"

I shook my head blankly. I couldn't remember her.

"Well, they took her off the train—she's in the hospital. Her arm was broken, but all you had was that bump on the head."

I raised my hand, but I couldn't feel any bandage.

7

"Better not touch it," the woman advised briskly. "The doctor saw to it and said it wouldn't give you any trouble. He'll be in to have another look at you before we change at Albury. But whatever in the world were you girls doing, moving heavy baggage around in the middle of the night?"

"I don't know," I said, staring at her.

"You must have been trying to pull them down from the upper bunk—was that it? And I suppose the train gave a jerk, and those two great suitcases landed down on the two of you. It was a nasty accident."

"How long have I been sleeping?" I asked, feeling frightened again, although I didn't exactly know why.

"Ever since you hurt yourself. The doctor gave you something. I was the one who found you two girls. I was going along to the—well, you know—and I heard her moaning. Miss Peters, that would be. You're Miss Ballister, aren't you? Cleo Ballister. There was a snapshot of you in your bag. Anyway, I came in, and you were both cramped up on the floor. She had her arm twisted under her, and she lost consciousness when she saw me."

I thought vaguely, *It was probably the purple robe.*

"I ran out to get help," the woman continued, "and luckily there was a doctor on the train. He telegraphed ahead to the next stop for an ambulance, and they carried Miss Peters off. You seemed to be all right, so he taped up that cut on your head and gave you something to make you sleep. We thought someone ought to stay with you, though, so I've been here ever since."

I said, "Thank you," rather uncertainly, and then there was a hearty bang at the door and it was flung open.

A man whom I took to be the doctor came in and said cheerfully, "Well, young lady, how now?" He bent over me, pulled something off my head and some of my hair out, and murmured, "Good, good—you won't have any trouble with that. I'll put a bit of tape there to protect it, and you can rip it off in a couple of days. Head ache a bit? Take an aspirin or two."

"Yes, I—it does. But I—feel a bit vague—I don't quite know—"

"Oh, that's all right," he said, still cheerful. "You let Mrs. Bunton here help you to dress, and as soon as we're in at Albury you can have a spot of tea. You'll feel quite the thing when you get some hot tea."

Tea? For breakfast?

He said, "Nice day," to Mrs. Bunton and breezed out before she could get a word in edgewise.

However, she took it in good part and said composedly, "Well, I'll get along to me own room now. You stay where you are, and I'll be back to help you dress when I'm right meself."

I said "Yes" docilely, and she made her way out. I squinted at the telegraph poles, pulled the blankets up around my chin, and then closed my eyes and went off to sleep again.

"You'll have to get up now," said the voice of Mrs. Bunton, and I opened my eyes and saw that she was dressed, even to coat and hat. The ensemble was no better than the purple dressing-robe, but she didn't seem to mind, so I tried not to.

I was still dizzy, but with Mrs. Bunton's efficient help I managed to get into my clothes and pack and lock the heavy suitcase. We had barely finished when the train slowed into a station, and Mrs. Bunton stooped to peer out of the window. "Albury. Good. I could do with a cup of tea. I'll get the guard to help with your bag."

I drew a long breath and said, "I feel pretty well now. Was I unconscious long?"

"No—don't you remember? You weren't really unconscious at all— only dazed like—and when we asked you questions you got all excited, so the doctor gave you something to make you sleep, and you went off at once."

She bustled away, and I waited quietly until she came back with a conductor, who took my bag and carried it out to the platform, talking amiably as he went. Mrs. Bunton talked too, and neither stopped for the other, but they seemed to get along all right.

We went into a restaurant, and the conductor put the suitcase on the floor. "All right, lidies. Don't be too long over your tucker. The Spirit of Progress'll be leaving 'ere soon, pretending to be a train."

Mrs. Bunton said, "Thank you very much," and I asked, "What is he talking about? What is the Spirit of Progress?"

"Oh, that's what the Victorians call their fancy train to Melbourne. It's a bonzer train, all right— but the guard is a New South Wales man." She laughed heartily and then settled her hat, purse, and umbrella. "My husband says it's a disgrace the way we have to change trains all over Australia, simply because the states have different gauge tracks."

Australia?

Fear stirred in me again, but the tea arrived, and it was hot and strong. Mrs. Bunton disposed of two cups and then drew a long, satisfied breath.

"I feel much better, and I'm sure you do too. I'll just get a man to carry your bag, and then I think we'd better be getting onto the train."

The bag disposed of, we moved along the platform in the crowd, and Mrs. Bunton said vigorously, "It really is absurd, having to change trains between Sydney and Melbourne, but of course it's not our fault.

New South Wales has the standard-gauge tracks—four foot eight and a half. Victoria is at fault with the odd gauge—five foot three."

"I beg to differ, madam," said a man's voice stiffly.

Mrs. Bunton and I both looked around, but the crowd must have pushed him away, because he said no more to back up his argument.

"Victorian scum?" I suggested.

Mrs. Bunton laughed heartily and then said, "Shh."

The Spirit of Progress turned out to be quite a train. Leather seats in various colors, soft carpets, and fine wood paneling. We established ourselves in a blue compartment, and I began to fumble in my enormous red pocketbook for a cigarette.

Mrs. Bunton glanced at me and said, "No—this isn't a smoker. We can go back to the smoking-car later."

I dropped the gold cigarette case back into the pocketbook and stared out of the window. Mrs. Bunton and the other occupants of the compartment were busy arranging and rearranging the baggage, but I hardly noticed them. I watched the platform until it began to slide away, smoothly and noiselessly, and then I glanced down at my hands and saw that they were shaking, and I faced squarely, for the first time, the fact that I was terrified.

I could not remember who I was or where I was going.

Chapter Two
INKLINGS

I GRITTED MY TEETH and, staring into the passing scenery, made a determined effort to concentrate—but it was no use. The mists were as thick as ever, and nothing came through. Cleo Ballister—that's who I was, apparently.

The two men who occupied the compartment with us had been complaining about its being a nonsmoker, and they presently went off, already hauling out cigarettes and bound for some spot where smoking was permitted.

Mrs. Bunton said, "Good riddance," and then collected her pocketbook and patted her bosom. "Well, my dear, we might as well go in to breakfast."

I felt unpleasantly awash with strong tea, and she nodded at me understandingly. "You'll be wanting your coffee, eh?"

Coffee. Of course I wanted coffee—strong and hot—and perhaps that would clear the fog in my head.

"You Americans and your coffee," said Mrs. Bunton, "are just like we are with our tea. Australians must have their hot cup of tea." She laughed heartily and then composed her face and indicated, without being indelicate enough to say so, that she intended going to the ladies' room before she had her breakfast. She asked, merely by a raise of the eyebrows and a significant look, whether I wanted to go too—but I shook my head, so she bustled off alone.

American. I was an American traveling in Australia—and this woman, Mrs. Bunton, knew more about me than I did myself. But how had she found out? My pocketbook. Of course! I snatched at the great red-leather thing and opened it eagerly.

Cigarettes, change purse, three handkerchiefs, all soiled. Perfume, nail file, scissors, tape measure, huge compact complete with rouge and a lipstick. A zipper pocket containing papers, letters, an application for a driver's license in Sydney, a snapshot of me, and four one-pound notes.

I studied the snapshot, but it did not tell me anything. I merely stood beside a tree and smiled sweetly into the camera. I put it away and took out one of the letters, which was signed *Uncle Joe*. Uncle Joe said that *they* would be on tap to meet me at the station at Melbourne and were looking forward to it.

Mrs. Bunton returned at this point and hustled me off to the dining-car. I found that the coffee was pretty bad and certainly did nothing to clear up my head, but the food was what she would have called "bonzer," and I made a good meal. She was a good trencherman herself, and when she had finished at last, she sat back and moaned softly.

"Oh, life, I've eaten too much—and me sister with a meal all ready as soon as I get in."

"What time do we get to Melbourne?" I asked.

"Half-past eleven. You'll be excited, meeting your relatives for the first time, when you've never seen them before. Your Uncle Joe'll look a treat with a white carnation, a red rose, and a cornflower in his buttonhole." She laughed explosively and then seemed to decide that an explanation was in order. "You see, we had to go through all your things, to find out about your relatives, in case we had to notify somebody. It wasn't needed, as things went—but we weren't to know that. I'd never have read your letters out of idle curiosity."

"No, no—of course not," I murmured, and thought confusedly that since, apparently, I had never seen Uncle Joe, I might as well stop trying to remember him.

Mrs. Bunton sighed and heaved herself to her feet. "Well, come along, lovey, we'll get back to our seats."

We returned to our compartment, and Mrs. Bunton continued to chatter.

"Such a pretty girl, that poor friend of yours— with her brown curls and blue eyes. You're pretty too—you're a pair of good-looking girls. I fancy your hair's a bit lighter and your eyes a bit darker than hers."

The girl who had been traveling with me, the one who had broken her arm. I thought hysterically that she was lucky—it was better to break your arm than break your memory into a thousand pieces.

"One look at you, and I knew that you were both American," Mrs. Bunton said idly. "And she in the hospital. She's a long way from home, poor soul!"

On this melancholy observation she quite suddenly fell asleep, and I quickly opened my red pocketbook again and drew out the application for a driver's license.

Cleo Balloter, single, twenty-eight, brown hair, blue eyes, five feet four. Los Angeles, California. Movie star? I found myself smiling and looked at the brief heading: *Occupation: Actress!*

I gasped and leaned back in my seat. But how much of an actress was I? There were so many rungs on that ladder. At any rate, I was traveling first class.

But I was frightened again. The application had stirred no chord of memory whatever, and I thought wildly that I'd have to go to a doctor as soon as I got to Melbourne. I couldn't, somehow, tell Mrs. Bunton, kind as she had been to me—she'd make too much of it. But I'd have to tell these mysterious relatives when I got to Melbourne, and they could take me to a doctor. I wouldn't be able to go on this way—I couldn't stand it.

Mrs. Bunton snored gently, and I glanced up and tried to pull myself together. After all, it wouldn't help to get scared and hysterical. I'd had a bang on the head, and I'd lost my memory. It had happened to people before—I wasn't the only one—and probably everything would come all right again if I relaxed and didn't try to force it.

I decided to go carefully through the letters, and started with the one from Uncle Joe. He mentioned the odd buttonhole he intended to wear, so that I could identify him, and said that he was sorry they could not get all the way to Sydney to pick me up, but Aunt Esther had so many relatives in Melbourne that it had taken all their time, and they really had to be getting back to Perth. It was time I paid them a visit, and what did Sydney have that they hadn't? He'd bet it was a boy—and why didn't I tell them about him?

The next one was a love letter from Billy, and it was a bit mushy and fairly brief. It ended rather oddly: *The man I got for you will walk up when he sees you greeting your relatives. He ought to be satisfactory, and he's going all the way to Perth. Name's Clive Butler.*

There was another love letter signed Jimmy. Jimmy said he thought we ought to be married shortly after we reached Perth. *After all, such love as ours should* not *be denied. You know we were made for each other and ought to have a splendid life together traveling all over the world. There is no use in your trying to back away or make objections, because I assure you I* won't *be turned down on this.*

Too bad about him, I thought idly. *He must expect to be turned down, or he wouldn't he so threatening about it.*

There were no other personal letters, but I found some bills for clothes from a Sydney firm, apparently unpaid, and a bankbook showing a balance of a few pounds in a Sydney bank. It was not enough to pay the bills and I wondered a little anxiously if I were expecting further funds from California shortly. There was nothing else except my train ticket, and I put everything away again.

I leaned back in my seat, feeling dizzy and confused. I ought to be happy, I reflected wryly. I had two ardent beaux, and a man named Clive Butler to dance attendance on me all the way to Perth. It occurred to me that it was rather handsome of Billy to go to all that trouble. Apparently I had my relatives for company during the trip, and it would have seemed that I could either give up flirting for that short time or take a chance on my fellow passengers.

The two men returned to their seats in the compartment, talking earnestly together, and I pretended to be asleep. I remember hoping that they would not lay Mrs. Bunton's snores at my door, and then I really did fall asleep, for the next thing I knew, Mrs. Bunton was prodding me and yelling, "Wake up—we're in."

I started up and automatically began to search frantically for my memory, but it wasn't there, so I hunted for my suitcase instead.

I don't care if it never comes back, I thought angrily. *Maybe I'm better off without it. I'll start off with a clean slate and no regrets—and I won't bother going to any doctor, either.*

"Here you are," said Mrs. Bunton, battling with my suitcase.

I clutched the great, heavy suitcase and stumbled after Mrs. Bunton's broad back. We made our way onto the crowded platform, and almost at once Mrs. Bunton shrieked gleefully, "There he is! See the red, white, and blue flowers in his buttonhole? That must be your Uncle Joe!"

She hustled me over to a big man who stood with a little group of people, introduced us, explained about my accident, and then, before anybody could say anything, caught sight of someone she knew in the crowd, yelled cheerfully, and was off.

I had come to depend on her heavily, and for a moment I felt very forlorn and alone—but Uncle Joe enfolded me in his arms and planted a kiss on my forehead. "Welcome to the bosom of your family," he murmured with a certain amount of emotion, after which he held me off at arm's length and looked me over. "You *are* a bosker lass, aren't you? Well, come on and meet the rest of us."

But the rest of them had to wait, because at that moment a large young man loomed up between Uncle Joe and me and, gathering me into his arms, gave me a long kiss.

Chapter Three
MY NEW FAMILY

I SUBMITTED RATHER DAZEDLY to the embrace, and he presently released me and said with a hint of impatience, "Wake up, darling—I want to be introduced to your family."

Uncle Joe, looming at my right elbow, suddenly boomed, "What's all this?" and I turned to look at him helplessly.

"Well, I—"

The young man laughed.

"Clive Butler, sir. Cleo is in a bit of a dither because it was all so sudden—we're engaged. I was lucky enough to get away and I'm making the trip with you."

"Well, well, well!" said Uncle Joe explosively. "What a surprise. *What* a surprise." He winked at me and dug the chap in the ribs. "Knew it was a boy—didn't I say so? Come along, both of you, and meet the family."

There was Aunt Esther, who seemed to be the widow of Uncle Joe's brother; Aunt Esther's son, Wilfred; and Wilfred's wife, Mary. This pair had a daughter, Eileen, who seemed to be about twelve—and last to be introduced was a dark, good-looking, well-dressed man, loosely described as Cousin Jimmy. Actually it developed that he was a vague relation of Aunt Esther's and occasionally stayed with her in Perth. He glowered at me in such a menacing fashion that I decided he must be the Jimmy of the love letter.

Uncle Joe rounded us all up and announced that our train left at seven in the evening. "We'll go along to the hotel and have a bit of a wash-up, and then we can get lunch."

Clive Butler said, "Darling, I'm so sorry, but I've some things to attend to that will keep me busy all day. I'll meet you on the train. You don't mind?"

"No, no—that's quite all right," I murmured hastily. "You run along."

He gave me an odd smile and then stooped and kissed me lightly on the cheek. He whispered, "I think I'm going to enjoy this," and took himself off.

I stared after him and heard myself saying, "Red hair, brown eyes, tall—"

Cousin Jimmy spoke suddenly against my ear. "You girls are all alike. I'm better looking than he is—and anyway, don't forget that you have no choice—"

"Jimmy!" Uncle Joe roared. "Leave the girl alone. Come on now— I've got a cab here. Esther and Cleo and little Eileen and I will ride, and you others can take a tram. You'd better get a hump on—we'll meet you at the 'otel."

The cab started with a jerk that threw Aunt Esther and me backward and Uncle Joe and Eileen almost onto our laps. Aunt Esther righted herself, straightened her hat, and said, "Hotel."

"I didn't say 'otel," Uncle Joe protested.

"Yes, you did. Cleo, I understand you want to go shopping this afternoon."

"Oh no," I said quickly. "I—well, I have some unpaid bills, and I want to get them settled before I pile up any more debts. I—I suppose I'll be getting money from America—"

Aunt Esther raised her eyebrows. "Really? But I thought you were not expecting any more from that source."

I fell silent and wondered wildly what I was going to do. All those bills in my purse—no money, and none coming. And I couldn't expect relatives I hadn't even seen before to support me.

The child Eileen had been regarding me from grave blue eyes beneath a straight bang of dark hair. She said now, "Your fancy is very handsome."

Uncle Joe guffawed, and the kid gave him a dirty look.

Aunt Esther said, "Fiance, dear. Cleo, is your young man well to do?"

I considered it and decided that most people were poor anyway and probably he was too "No," I said, "but I expect we'll get along."

Aunt Esther frowned. "Of course you know your own mind best— but with your extravagant tastes—"

"Ah, bosh!" Uncle Joe snorted. "Leave the girl alone. What's money?"

"It's the difference between breaking your back over a washboard and having your breakfast in bed," Aunt Esther told him, in the tone of one who knew.

"Ah, go on, Esther—you were always one to whine about housework. There's nothing to it. Here, Cleo, give me all your bills, girl, and

I'll pay them. You can start afresh. You marry that doctor of yours, and never mind about the money—you'll get along."

"That's exactly what I did," Aunt Esther said thinly, "and I got along. My husband and I worked, but I struggled with a house and babies for twenty-four hours a day, while he spent his off time in the saloon, drinking up the money that would have provided a washwoman for me."

"Esther!" said Uncle Joe, looking deeply shocked. "Me poor brother Tom has passed on, and I always say, 'Peace be with the dead.' "

Eileen passed the remark that her husband would have to give her a million pounds before she'd marry him, and then the taxi came to a stop before the hotel.

Uncle Joe had a table reserved for our lunch, and he was in great fettle during the meal. He was pleased with my engagement and very anxious to know when the wedding was to be, but I had to tell him, in all honesty, that I did not know.

Jimmy, sending me a look from under his eyelashes, said, "She'll quarrel with Butler and break the whole thing off before we get to Perth."

"No, I won't," I declared, with a flash of spirit. I was in utter confusion about the whole thing, but at least it seemed probable that Clive Butler was a buffer between the threatening Jimmy and myself.

The lunch proceeded noisily. With the exception of Jimmy, everyone seemed cheerful, including even the hitherto dour Aunt Esther. She was a tall, thin woman, with only a few strands of gray in her dark hair, and I could not see that her son Wilfred resembled her in any way. He was inclined to be short and plump and had thinning sandy hair. He was more like a young edition of Uncle Joe, except that his upper lip was bare, while Uncle Joe sported a magnificent walrus mustache.

Wilfred's wife Mary was plump and suspiciously blond, and always told Wilfred what to do next. I thought the child Eileen was more interesting than either of her parents. She had assurance and intelligence, and there was something of her grandmother about her.

After lunch I was allowed to go up to Aunt Esther's room and lie down. Uncle Joe wanted me to go shopping with him—he declared the shopping was much better in Melbourne than in Perth—but the two women reminded him of my accident, so he gave up and took Eileen instead.

Aunt Esther and Mary came with me, and I very nearly told them of my predicament—and then, somehow, I didn't. I stretched out gratefully on the bed, and after Mary had covered me with a blanket I drifted off to sleep with the thought that perhaps when I woke up my mind would be clear again. The last thing I heard was Esther's voice saying worriedly, "Well, I don't see how he can spend too much with only Eileen to inspire him.

So I dreamed of Eileen shopping with Uncle Joe, and I had got to the part where she'd bought a mink coat that was much too big for her—and was flopping her arms up and down with the sleeves hanging over her hands, when Aunt Esther shook me vigorously by the shoulder and said, "Cleo! Cleo, wake up! We've only just time to get to the train."

She was wrong, as it turned out. We reached the station half an hour before the train was due to leave and stood around in a family circle bickering about what we ought to do to fill in the time. I realized at about this time, and somewhat to my dismay, that Jimmy was coming with us. I had hoped, and believed, that he was staying in Melbourne.

"I *knew* we should have had our dinner before getting on the train," Mary fretted. "Now it will be after Eileen's bedtime before we finish, and I always make a point of getting her to bed by eight o'clock."

"I'm *not* going to bed before I've had my dinner," said the kid firmly.

"Now, then," Uncle Joe interposed, "stop grousing, Mary. How could we all gulp our dinners down right after tea? And then sit and starve on the train all night?"

"For God's sake," Jimmy muttered, "do we have to stand out here in the middle of the station yelling about it?"

"All right, old boy," Wilfred said vaguely. "No need to get shifty."

"Well, well, well, 'ere's your boy!" Uncle Joe bellowed suddenly.

"Here's your boy," said Aunt Esther.

I turned quickly and watched the approach of Clive Butler, while I struggled with the question of why he had been so generously provided by the unknown Billy.

He came up, tall and tanned and good-looking, and smiled at me. "Why so serious?" he asked casually. He put an arm across my shoulders and glanced around at the others. "Suppose we get on the train?"

Jimmy gave him an oblique look and asked nastily, "Who was the girl you were with this afternoon? Saw you on Collins Street." Clive dropped his arm from my shoulders, cleared his throat, and then found nothing to say.

I surprised myself by trilling brightly, "That was Amy Drummond, Jim. Clive was trying to sell her insurance. Clive is the poor son of poor parents, but he's bound and determined to get to the top. He has a lot of potential customers, and—"

I stopped short and thought wildly that not only had I lost my memory but I'd gone a bit silly too. Or maybe I was naturally silly—I had no way of knowing.

The others were laughing at me. "She really loves him," Mary said indulgently as we all began to move toward the train.

Clive picked up my suitcase and walked me off ahead. "Thanks for the rescue," he murmured, and, sounded amused. "But you tripped up badly on my parents. They were the richest people in Sale for many years."

"Sale?"

"It's a town—a young up-and-coming city."

"Near Perth?"

"No, in Victoria. Near the sea."

"Oh," I said. "You're native Victorian scum, then?"

"I'm *what!*" he yelled.

But I hardly heard him. I had stepped into the train, and as I stood there the mists in my mind parted briefly and I got the first confused, tantalizing glance back into my past.

The car was exactly like an American Pullman, and I immediately saw myself in another American Pullman in the company of an elderly woman who wore a white suit.

Chapter Four
PLENTY OF IMAGINATION

I STOOD QUITE STILL as the vague picture drifted through my mind, but somehow the more desperately I sought to clear it, the fainter it seemed to grow. I was left, at last, with only an impression that the woman had made a mistake in wearing the white linen suit, since it had soiled too quickly.

My relatives were pushing behind me, and at last I gave it up and moved on—but I felt considerably cheered. If little wisps of remembrance were beginning to break through, then surely it could not be long before my mind was clear and normal again.

It immediately developed that all our reservations were not adjacent, but seemed to be scattered here and there along the train—and Uncle Joe was upset about it. "I know things are crowded now, but I should think they could have got us close together."

"Oh, stop making a fuss about nothing," Aunt Esther said impatiently. "What difference does it make? You sound just like George. He never could travel without finding something to grouse about."

"George's only been gone for five months," Uncle Joe said, looking shocked. "A little respect wouldn't hurt."

Aunt Esther settled herself into her seat and observed, "It wouldn't do him any good, either. You be respectful, Joe. I needn't bother—he didn't leave me any money."

Wilfred heard this and swung around with his face reddening. "Mother!"

Aunt Esther ignored him and picked up a magazine. "I'm tired, and I want my dinner as soon as possible. I want to go to bed."

She retired into her magazine, and Uncle Joe flitted off busily, as though he were the conductor of a tour. He could be heard, presently, having a row with one of the trainmen because Clive's accommodations were two carriages up. I heard Clive say, "Please don't worry about it, Mr. Ballister. I've only to sleep there—I can sit with Cleo during the day—and when I'm sleeping I'm not much company anyway."

I relaxed into my seat and reflected idly that since Uncle Joe and I bore the same name, he must be my father's brother. But who was my father? Did he look like Uncle Joe? No. Very definitely, he did not. It was another flash of memory, but it didn't help me much. I knew only that my father did not look anything like Uncle Joe.

Jimmy had disappeared, and I found that Eileen was sitting opposite me. She looked so cross that I roused myself and made an effort to be pleasant.

"Did you have a good time today?" I asked.

The freckled nose and sulky mouth broke into a definite sneer. "Good time!" she said scornfully. "I should say not! Uncle Joe took me to see Father Christmas—actually."

"Father Christmas?" I murmured vaguely.

"Santa Claus," she translated impatiently.

"Oh well," I agreed, "he ought to know better than that."

The child sighed in an exasperated fashion. "But I have to be nice to Uncle Joe," she stated simply. "He has money, you see."

"Who—er—told you to be nice to him because he has money?"

"Mother," she said, without bothering to blush.

We all went along to the dining-car presently, and I was seated at a table with Clive, Aunt Esther, and Uncle Joe—which was Uncle Joe's arrangement. He also did most of the talking, and told us about a bygone gold rush at Kalgoorlie which he had attended without success. Twice, at least, he took time out to tell me how glad he was that I had come and how he hoped I would stay with them always.

Immediately after dinner Eileen was put to bed, which seemed to be a major operation. Clive had disappeared, but Jimmy sidled up and asked if I'd like to go along to the recreation car and have a smoke.

I agreed gratefully, and we made our way through the train and arrived finally at a lounge car, where, to my embarrassment and his, Clive loomed as the sole occupant.

Jimmy grinned. "Hello, old man—so this is where you are. Thought I'd take care of Cleo, since you seemed to have done a bunk."

"Er—thanks," Clive murmured. "Nice of you. We had a tiff—lovers' quarrel, you know."

"Good," said Jimmy, "then we don't have to sit with you—we'll go on down to the end. And I hope you don't crawl up asking forgiveness too soon. If I were you, Cleo, I wouldn't give in too easily—it's a bad basis for married life."

"You've got that wrong," Clive called after us. "I'm waiting for her to make the first move."

Jimmy assumed a sneer that was startlingly reminiscent of the kid Eileen. He said scornfully, "You know she's an American, don't you? They never ask pardon, no matter how wrong they are. You can believe me, cobber—I've had experience. If that's what you're waiting for, you'll sit there until your bottom grows to the chair."

Clive stood up at once and brushed off his so-called bottom. "You alarm me," he said, and began to make his way toward us.

"You can't sit here," I said coldly. "Not until you apologize."

He bowed from the waist and Murmured, "Please forgive me—I was wrong."

"And you won't fuss any more about allowing my relations to live with us?"

"You may fill the house with them, and I'll stretch out in the chicken run with the hens."

"All right," I said. "Sit down, then."

Jimmy scowled and muttered, "It rings false."

I shrugged, and Clive laughed, and at that moment Uncle Joe entered the car, still looking as fresh and rosy as when I had first seen him that morning.

"Well, well, well," he boomed. "Here you are, then. 'Ow goes it?"

"How," Jimmy murmured under his breath.

"Splendid," said Clive. "Come on and have a yarn with us."

But Uncle Joe knew all about two being company and three a crowd under certain circumstances, and while he shook his head his eye fell on Jimmy and gleamed with sudden purpose.

"Come on, young feller-me-lad—I've been looking for you. Esther's suitcase is stuck, and we can't get it open. Her night shift is in it, and she wants to go to bed."

Jimmy got to his feet and threw Clive and me a parting look that was faintly evil. "I'll be back in a jiff," he said, almost with warning.

"Two jiffs will be all right," Clive replied.

Uncle Joe roared with laughter and then patted my shoulder. "Have your fun, girl."

I looked after Jimmy rather wistfully. In a way he was my only link with the past, the only one of them who had ever seen me before my accident. At least I knew—through his having known me before—that I was Cleo Ballister. He was fond of me, too—even if his love-letters were a bit odd. I turned to Clive and was astonished to find that his social temperature had dropped to zero. His jaw was a grim line and his eyes cold and unfriendly.

"What's the matter now?" I asked helplessly. "Are you worrying about sleeping out with the hens?"

"No." His voice was flat and cold. "I'm thinking about poor old Bill."

"Oh, yes," I muttered. "Bill. Why don't you write him and warn him?"

"I wouldn't mind, if things were the way he thought—that you were afraid of this Jimmy—but you're not. You're openly flirting with him and using him to promote more interest in yourself. I suppose that sort of thing is all you ever think of."

"Seems to me I don't have to bother thinking of it," I said flippantly. "Two men who want me, and a third—yourself—about to fall in love with me. I wonder why I'm so fascinating."

"If you're asking me," he replied coolly, "I wouldn't know. Take a look at yourself in that mirror over there."

I glanced at the mirror—narrow, but reaching almost to the floor—and with a little flash of anger I got up and went and stood directly in front of it.

I skipped my face, which I had seen on and off all day in the little mirror in my purse, and took a good look at the rest of me—and I was appalled.

I wore a gray suit which was slightly soiled, a gray sweater, white pearls, red hat with a red veil, and red shoes. The shoes had been hurting me all day, and the suit was skintight.

"Oh God!" I moaned. "What taste!"

I crept away from the mirror and sat down again. I *couldn't* have bought and assembled these clothes—they must have belonged to that other girl—someone had switched our suitcases after the accident. I twisted my hands together in my lap and tried despairingly to remember what I had been wearing, but I could not get a glimmer. I had only a rebellious conviction that it was not the awful things I had on now.

I raised my eyes to find Clive regarding me rather oddly. "What's frightening you? I believe your teeth are actually chattering. Reminds me of the way I felt when I went to work on my first cadaver."

Cadaver? "Oh," I gasped, "are you a doctor?"

He nodded.

"The best doctor in Sale, maybe?"

"Maybe not."

"Well, never mind that," I said impatiently. "I need your help. I've been a fool, I guess. I should have seen a doctor in Melbourne—only I kept thinking it would clear up. I didn't tell the others, because I thought I'd start to remember things when I talked to them. Only I didn't. You see, I've never seen them before—I—"

"Come to the point and stop dithering," he said shortly.

I rested my head against the back of the chair and closed my eyes. I wanted to cry, but I wouldn't cry in front of him. After a moment I said almost steadily, "I had an accident last night and hit my head—and I've lost my memory, completely. I can't remember anything or anybody."

There was a moment's silence, and then Clive laughed. "I'll give you this much," he said. "You have plenty of imagination. Only I'm not sure that this isn't going a bit beyond the odds. What do you expect to get out of it, anyway?"

I sat there quite quietly, my heart in a whirl. So he didn't believe me—and how could I possibly prove it?

I heard him get up from his seat, and he said, "You'll excuse me, I'm sure, if I leave you and go to bed. You can sit there and think up something new for tomorrow."

I flung out of my chair and caught up with him. "Wait a minute. If you thought I really meant these poisonous clothes, you wouldn't have told me to look at myself. So why did you do it?"

He lifted his shoulders and said, "Well, you have a point there, of course. Damn rude of me, if I *had* thought you meant those clothes. But perhaps you assembled them for Jimmy."

"Not Jimmy—never—and you know it. Uncle Joe, perhaps—or maybe Bill—told me you were a Sale boy, and I figured anyone with straw sticking out of his ears would go for red shoes."

He turned away abruptly and said, "Leave Sale out of it."

"All right, dear," I sighed. "It shall not cross my unworthy lips again."

He pretended not to hear and strode on ahead.

When we reached my carriage we found it already half curtained off and a goodly collection of my relatives standing in a group, blocking the aisle. Aunt Esther's suitcase appeared to have been opened, but she, Uncle Joe, and Jimmy stood staring at each other. As we approached, Uncle Joe said, "But Jimmy, how could I have finished painting that little lizard without even knowing I did it?"

Chapter Five
THE SPOILED PAINTING

AUNT ESTHER TURNED AND SAW US and said quickly, "Never mind about it, Joe—it's all right. Close the suitcase and shove it under the seat. I have my things."

But Uncle Joe continued to bark. "Where's my suitcase? I'm going to look at that painting. Where is it, Esther? My suitcase? Where's it been put?"

Aunt Esther sighed and sat down. She indicated Uncle Joe's suitcase, under his seat across the aisle from her own, and fell to studying her nails in silence.

Clive cleared his throat and said, "Well, good night, everybody. I'm off to bed."

Aunt Esther and I murmured, "Good night," and Jimmy made a face. Uncle Joe was grunting over his suitcase. He pulled a small block from one of the back pockets as Clive went off, and studied it in an absorbed fashion.

"What is it, Uncle Joe?" I asked, looking over his shoulder.

The thing was badly done in water colors—a small lizard reposing on bright green grass.

Uncle Joe put it down at last and turned to the other two, his face mottled with angry red and his voice rough. "Now then—who did it, eh? Who mucked my work about like that?"

Aunt Esther and Jimmy gazed back at him in silence, and the veins began to stand out on his forehead. His voice rose as he held the thing practically under their noses. "Look at it, will you?"

"Shh," said Aunt Esther hastily. "There are people sleeping here. All right, somebody else did it. Now do put it away."

Uncle Joe swung around to glare at Jimmy, who shrugged and smoothed his already smooth hair.

"What is it? What's the matter?" I asked.

25

Uncle Joe turned to me, apparently happy to unload his grievance into a sympathetic ear.

"I've been working on this little painting, Cleo, and I told Esther, and Jimmy, here, that I was going to take it out and finish it as soon as we get to Adelaide—and they turn around and tell me I've already finished it. I knew I hadn't finished it—so I get it out, and look what's happened to it! Somebody's mucked about with it and spoiled it. I couldn't have messed it up like that—even in my sleep."

"Somebody has played a joke on you," I said, trying to be sympathetic. "It looks as though it might be Eileen's work."

He shook his head, while Aunt Esther and Jimmy remained silent. "Eileen can't paint anything, not even a botch like this."

Aunt Esther stirred and said, "Go to bed, Joe. I'll get them to make up your berth as soon as mine's done."

"Well—but I don't like it. I don't understand it."

Jimmy moved to my side and said, "Come on back to the lounge car again, Cleo, and let's have a yarn. I've something to tell you."

I shook my head. "I'm going to bed—I'm dead. I had that accident last night, you know."

He turned away with a shrug, and I went to my berth, which was already made up, with Eileen sleeping in the upper. I felt tired and confused, and my head was spinning a little. I opened my suitcase, and after tumbling it around I found a pale blue silk nightgown with a matching chiffon robe. That was all right, but the bedroom slippers irritated me. They were of rainbow brocade and badly soiled.

Aunt Esther accompanied me to the ladies' dressing-room and chatted amiably while we undressed.

"It's nice having you come to stay with us for a while—I'm sure you'll like Perth. It's hot at Christmas time, of course—but not too bad. I'll give you a small room upstairs, if you don't mind, because I have the others rented now and I don't want to put any of the boarders out."

A boarding-house. I said hastily, "Oh, of course—I'd rather have a small room, anyway. I'd like the least expensive—"

"My dear, you're not going to pay—you're Joe's guest. He's paying me for your board, and he wanted the best room in the house for you—but I'm sure you'll understand It would mean putting somebody out, and that's bad for business."

"No, no—you mustn't do that. I'll tell Uncle Joe I much prefer a small room."

She gave a sigh of relief and glanced at me gratefully, and after a moment's silence I asked, "What was all that fuss about the painting?"

She made a vexed sound and shook her head. "I'm sure I don't know. He talks about finishing the painting tomorrow—and I'm sure he finished it this morning. He must be getting old—although he's only fifty-eight. I'm sixty-four, and I'm sure I have all my wits about me."

I made a conventional remark of surprise and protest which seemed to please her, and we presently made our way back through the narrow aisle to our berths. She told me that Mary and Wilfred had been very tired and had gone to bed immediately after dinner, and then we said good night and I crawled into my bed.

I could not sleep, though. I kept thinking of Uncle Joe, who painted a picture in the morning and forgot about it by evening, and I wondered whether he was quite right in the head. But then I wasn't quite right in the head myself, so who was I to criticize?

I turned my face into the pillow and cried for some time, and when at last I dried off I felt more relaxed. Perhaps I had better tell the family what was wrong with me, I reflected, and they could take me to a doctor in Adelaide.

I turned restlessly and raised the window shade. We seemed to be passing through a small town—something comparable to Sale, perhaps, I thought, and laughed quietly. I ought not to bandy Sale around in my degraded mind.

I wondered why Clive was going to Western Australia when his home was in Victoria. And why on earth was he pretending to be engaged to me? I shouldn't have allowed it—I should never have got into the thing. As far as I could make out, it had been Bill's idea to keep Jimmy at bay. But surely I wasn't such a poor weak sister that I couldn't handle Jimmy's love-making!

I turned on the little light at my head and got out Bill's letter again. I gathered that at present he was working in Brisbane, but though I strained my mind to the utmost, I could not picture him. Instead the elderly woman in the white linen suit drifted into my consciousness again. I seemed to remember lying in a berth on a train, just as I was now, and the woman had put her head through the curtains and said, "Here, have an aspirin and you'll feel better."

I could not get any more, but I went off to sleep with a satisfied feeling that it was another breakthrough into the past.

The train was not so smooth as the Victorian Spirit of Progress had been, but I managed to sleep pretty well. Once I woke to hear Aunt Esther out of her berth and speaking in a low, soothing voice to Uncle Joe. She said, "It's all right, we're not on the Nullarbor Plain yet—there are trees all around."

I stuck my head out of my curtain, and she turned and smiled at me. "Joe must have been having a nightmare. He was muttering about there being no trees around and he couldn't feed his little lizard."

"His little lizard!" I repeated, shivering.

"Where does he keep it?"

She laughed at me. "Don't worry. He's been having a nightmare."

She crept back into her berth, which was below Jimmy's, and I drifted off to sleep again. But the next time I awoke it was with some remnant of a dream about a lizard. I found myself uneasily searching through the bedclothes before I was clear enough to remember that it was only a painted lizard. And even then I lay there stupidly wondering why Uncle Joe had made his lizard so dark. Weren't they usually greenish or bluish? At that point I woke up entirely and told myself to stop dreaming and go back to sleep again.

Mary woke me in the morning with a warning to hurry, because we were due in at 8:25. I glanced at my wristwatch and was diverted by the reflection that it appeared to be a valuable piece of jewelry, and in quiet taste. Why did I have such a satisfactory watch, then—and such terrible clothes? I must have the other girl's clothes, and I'd simply have to get in touch with her in some way.

I realized suddenly that the hands of the watch stood at a quarter past seven—and I had over an hour to dress. I struggled into the chiffon robe and the ugly slippers, collected my washing-bag, and went out into the aisle, where I crashed into Clive.

He steadied me with his arm and looked me over.

"Not so bad this morning," he conceded.

"Let me past," I said. "I've only an hour and five minutes to get dressed."

"An hour and thirty-five minutes," he said without moving. "I suppose you forgot to put your watch back at the border."

"What border?"

"Victoria and South Australia. You should have put your watch back thirty minutes."

"Oh," I said. "So we eeled out of Victoria last night. I thought the air seemed fresher."

"Get yourself dressed. I hope you have another costume with you. If you have, we might breakfast together."

"Oh, I do thank you," I said humbly. "I shall get another costume if I have to steal one."

"Cleo, do hurry! You'll never be ready in time," Mary's worried voice called.

Clive glanced at his watch and said, "Don't break a leg. The train's bound to be a few minutes late."

I flew through my washing and hair combing and then hurried

back to my berth. The suitcase yielded up a set of clean underthings, which I thankfully put on, but the problem of another costume was a bit more difficult. The weather was noticeably warmer, but a thorough search through the suitcase turned up a lone silk dress—a print of violent green and red, with two huge rhinestone pins attached to the neck. Apparently the red in the print was supposed to match the shoes, hat, and bag—the green being merely thrown in for good measure.

I shook my head and turned back to the suit. I found that the skirt was less soiled than the coat, so I put it on with the sweater—which was quite clean. I had to use the shoes and pocketbook, but after I had jammed the suit-coat, the red hat, and the white pearls back into the suitcase I felt that I didn't look so bad after all. I finished my packing and lit a cigarette.

The kid Eileen wandered along and looked me over. "Where's your hat and coat, Auntie?" she asked critically.

"Too hot for a hat and coat."

"But you can't change trains without a hat," the kid persisted. "Not a grown-up lady like you. And you don't look very dressed up with just a jersey on. Why don't you have a blouse?"

I moved over to an empty seat and she followed, still looking distressed. "This is Uncle Joe's seat," she said. "He's been up for hours."

I looked out of the window. Bright, flooding sunlight and beautiful country. But who was I?

"You must be that lady who stayed with us last winter when Uncle George died," Eileen said quietly.

Chapter Six
REDHEADED WOMAN

I STARED AT THE KID for a moment and then gasped, "What do you mean?"

She leaned closer to me and dropped her voice to a whisper. "You had your hair dyed red, didn't you? Mother kept saying it was never natural—that red hair. Nobody would know you the way you are, though. I wouldn't. You just don't look a bit like you did when you had that red hair."

"But—then how do you know I am the same person?"

She wrinkled her freckled nose, and the whisper became more conspiratorial. "The lucky penny, of course. Don't you remember how you told me you'd never be parted from that penny—never, even for a day—and nobody else in the world had one just like it? See?" She pointed to my pocketbook.

I looked down and noticed for the first time an American penny that seemed to have been made into a brooch and was pinned to the outside of the red bag. There was a nick out of one side of it, and it needed polishing.

I looked at Eileen helplessly, but before either one of us had time to say anything more her mother called her and she tripped away.

I looked down at the bag and the ugly-looking brooch that was made out of a penny. I had been convinced that I had that other girl's clothes—but was the bag hers or mine? It seemed certain that it had been bought to match the red shoes and hat, and yet it contained the snapshot of me and the letters from Uncle Joe and Jimmy. I shook my head, feeling cross and confused. Whatever was the explanation of the clothes, I must have bought the bag myself and used it. And it had a lucky penny pinned to it, which seemed to mean that I had spent the previous winter in Perth, in Aunt Esther's boardinghouse, disguised as a strawberry blonde.

We were drawing into the station at Adelaide, and Wilfred came bustling excitedly down the aisle.

"Come along, Cleo—we've collected all the luggage down at the end. Come along, my dear—don't get lost."

I reflected that he'd be startled if he knew how lost I really was, but I followed him in silence to the end of the car. With the exception of Jimmy, they were all clustered about the luggage, apparently waiting on tenterhooks until the door should be opened and they could make a safe landing—although they all knew that Adelaide was the end of the line.

Uncle Joe looked up at me and went into a panic immediately. "Your 'at and coat! You haven't got your 'at and coat! Quick, somebody—find her 'at and coat!"

"Hat," said Aunt Esther.

I had to shout an explanation that it was too hot for a hat and coat and I'd packed them.

Mary clicked her tongue and said, "Oh dear, I'm afraid you'll look a bit odd without your hat, at least."

"Why?" I asked. "Am I bald or something?"

Mary looked at me blankly, but Eileen and Uncle Joe went off into peals of laughter.

Aunt Esther said, "Rubbish! They can't arrest the girl for going without a hat."

Jimmy sauntered up and deposited his suitcase with the rest. "We're only about fifteen minutes late," he observed. "We could take a stroll around the town."

"Don't be absurd!" Wilfred exclaimed fretfully. "We've only half an hour to change from this train to the other."

"Take us all of that to cross the platform, I suppose," Jimmy said sarcastically. "How about it, Cleo—want to take a walk? Adelaide's a pretty place."

Mary started to make a heated remark of some sort, but the train stopped as she started, and there ensued a mad rush. In nothing flat we were all seated in a compartment in the other train—including Clive, who had added himself to us at some point in the proceedings. The compartment was hardly large enough for us, but it was decided, in a sort of general discussion, that it would be better for us to stick together since it was only a short run.

"But I thought it was quite a long distance from Adelaide to the west coast of Australia, I said in some confusion.

"This only goes to Port Pirie," Uncle Joe explained. "We change to the Trans-Australian there. It's quite a run, that, including three hundred and thirty miles of straight stretch."

"You'll see it all for yourself," Jimmy said, putting an urgent hand on my arm. "Come on, let's have a bit of a walk—see something of Adelaide. I had a girl named Adelaide once."

I went out onto the platform with him, and we began to walk slowly in the direction of the street.

"I'm sure you've had girls of all shapes and sizes," I said absently, "but to get back to this train changing. I mean, how many more times do we have to? It seems to me ridiculous that you can't get from the east coast to the west without changing trains practically in your sleep."

"Old American Efficiency," said a voice behind us, and I turned to behold Clive and Uncle Joe. "We're coming too," Clive went on. "Don't mind, do you?"

Jimmy said, "Yes, I do," and Uncle Joe let out a horselaugh.

"Well, you 'ave got a cheek. Trying to take a man's sweetheart away from him in front of his face."

"You'd do it behind his back, I suppose," Jimmy suggested. "I'm the decent kind."

The station was large, and I thought it quite an impressive building. As a matter of fact, it was about all I was destined to see of Adelaide, for the sun was very hot, and since I wore no 'at, Uncle Joe made it his business to see that I stayed in the shade.

"Can't monkey around with Australian sun," he warned me. "And anyway, we must keep an eye on the train. Don't want to get left behind."

I watched the street idly, wishing that somewhere, sometime, I could come upon a scene that was familiar to me.

A car approached, and as it passed I said suddenly, "Why, that's mine—it's my car."

Uncle Joe gazed at its retreating back, pushing his hat to the back of his head and squinting into the sun. "Buick," he said. "But, look here, Cleo— I thought you'd sold all your gear?"

"Well, I—yes—but I had a car like that."

I had, too—it was another flash of memory—and I felt a vague sorrow that I had apparently disposed of it.

I became conscious of perspiration on my forehead and my upper lip, and I rolled up the sleeves of the gray sweater. As we made our way back to the train I wished irritably that I had thought of buying a thin, cool dress.

"I'd give a lot to know who's been messing about with me paints," Uncle Joe was saying. "Someone finished that little lizard, and finished it in more ways than one, and I'd like to get to the bottom of it. I don't like people mucking into me paints."

"Don't you think Eileen—"

"No," he interrupted me. "I tried to get the youngster to learn painting, but she says she's going to be an actress like her Auntie Cleo."

He winked at me and laughed heartily, and I preened a little. "It's hard work," I murmured.

"When you get it," Jimmy said caustically.

I deflated at once. Only a ham actress apparently, I thought, and was disappointed.

We walked back through the spacious station and met Wilfred, who was frantically searching for us.

"Hurry! For heaven's sake, hurry!" he cried. "We've only five minutes!"

Behind me Clive murmured, "Tch, tch, I shall have to cut corners. It usually takes me ten minutes to step on a train."

Eileen met us in the corridor of the car and said accusingly, "Mother and Grandma were sure you would miss the train." Her eye fell on me, and she added, "Auntie, why don't you pull down your sleeves?"

"You can't walk around in America," I explained, "with the sleeves of your sweater pulled down. It just isn't done. All the girls pull them up—to the elbow or above."

And they did, too. I knew it quite definitely, without knowing how I knew it. It gave me a buoyant feeling that bits of memory were poking through all the time, now, and surely I'd soon be back to normal.

Eileen was somewhat dashed but still not quite convinced. She said doubtfully, "It's not exactly the fashion here, though."

"It will be," I assured her. "When people see me wearing my sleeves this way, it'll get about."

The kid dropped my sleeves and, taking a significant look at my skirt, passed the remark that it was a bit tight.

Mary called out, "Eileen! It's very rude to make personal remarks. Don't let me hear you doing it again."

Eileen closed her mouth, but her expression indicated that her opinion was unchanged. She silently made way for Jimmy in the narrow corridor, and he sidled up to me with a suggestion that we go along to the dining-saloon and get breakfast. "There are things we must discuss. I can't ever get you alone, and I'm getting a bit fed up with it. I might begin to talk out of pure boredom—and that wouldn't suit your book, would it?"

I glanced into our compartment and saw that the others were all arguing as to whether they should go to breakfast in a body or break it up into two shifts, so that the luggage would not be left alone. Clive was in the thick of it, quite as though he were one of the family.

I nodded to Jimmy, and we slipped off and made our way to the diner. We were given a nice table, and I sat back and decided to forget my worries. I might as well have a pleasant time with this Jimmy, who was full of unaccountable insinuations.

"Tell me about the redheaded widow who stayed with your Aunt Esther last winter," I suggested brightly. "Quite something, wasn't she?"

Jimmy slitted his eyes and said coldly, "Come off it—that wasn't so good. You could spot that the hair was dyed at ten yards."

Chapter Seven
A PIECE OF STRING

SO I *was* the redheaded woman. But what conceivable reason could I have had for going to live at Aunt Esther's boarding-house—incognito, and with my hair dyed?

I extracted the little mirror from the vast red pocketbook and looked closely at my hair, but certainly there was no trace of dye on it.

Jimmy had been watching me in silence, and he said now, "That was a stupid move—that red hair—it attracted attention to you. Anyway, that's all water under the bridge now, and no one seems to be any the wiser—except, of course, myself." He leaned back in his chair and shook his head a little. "I'll give you this much—I've never seen downright, crass cheek like yours."

"You like that?"

He looked at me from under lowered eyelids and laughed. "I love it—and I love you. And you might bear in mind that, without any further dangerous fooling about, we are to be married in the near future. It's like your brazen impudence to produce this Clive fellow in an effort to sidetrack me, but I'm not that easily pushed around. I don't know what your grouse is, anyway. What's the matter with me?"

"I don't know," I said honestly. "Nothing, I'm sure. But look—what was so dangerous about my calling attention to myself with that red hair?"

He had opened his mouth to reply, and I was waiting eagerly to hear what little more about myself might be forthcoming, when Clive strolled into the car, followed by the rest of the family. They piled right up to our table and wanted to know what on earth we were doing here.

Jimmy said he didn't know, unless it could be that we were having breakfast, and Mary patiently begged him not to be silly. They found seats all around us, and Uncle Joe and Clive took the other two at our table.

Uncle Joe shook his walrus mustache at me and winked. "Cleo, girl, I'm afraid you're a bit of a flirt."

"Cleo and I find we have a lot in common," Jimmy said, looking bored. He glanced at Clive and added, "You don't mind?"

"Not at all," Clive said largely. "Not at all."

Uncle Joe eyed him. "You Victorians. You're more like the pommies than they are themselves."

"Pommies?" I asked, looking from one to the other.

"The English," Clive translated, with a touch of impatience. "Anyway, I deny it. I was born and bred in Sale. I'm a product of Sale, and we Sale people don't copy anybody."

"How many Sale people are there?"

Clive fingered his teaspoon and hedged. "Er—what exactly do you mean?"

"Exactly, then, I mean what is the population?"

"Oh," he said. "Yes—the population. It's growing all the time, you know—by leaps and bounds, really. I think I'd be safe in saying that in a very few years—"

"Now, I interrupted firmly. "I want the population as of today."

He stared out of the window at the passing scenery and said bravely, "Four thousand five hundred."

I sat back and laughed for some time. The richest boy in a town of 4500. It was anybody's guess.

"What's the population of your home town? If you can stop sneering at Sale long enough to tell me."

"Fairly modest," I said, and wondered hollowly whether I would ever again be able to name my home town. "It might be a million or two."

"You ought not to rub his nose in the dirt too hard, girl," Uncle Joe interposed. "Remember, he's going to be your husband. Not that I wouldn't take a dig or two at that little bump on the map he hails from— only I'm not engaged to him."

Clive turned on him. "Why should you cast aspersions on Sale?"

"I'm a New South Wales man," Uncle Joe explained. "Born in Sydney."

"Oh," said Clive, "Sydney."

"Whaddaya mean, 'Oh, Sydney'?" Uncle Joe demanded hotly.

"Tell me something," I broke in pacifically. "Why do the two states have different gauge tracks? It seems downright absurd to have to change trains when you're traveling between the two largest cities in Australia."

I had intended to restore peace, but instead I started a squabble that looked at one time as though it might wreck the diner.

Clive started off first, with Victoria's side of the story. "Victoria," he stated loudly, "wanted to have the standard four-foot-eight track, but New South Wales said no, five three. They were so determined about it that Victoria started building five three—only to wake up, one fine morning, and find New South Wales busily laying tracks with a four-eight-and-a-half gauge—"

I don't believe he ever got any farther than that. Jimmy and Uncle Joe gave their versions, and then some people sitting at the table behind us leaped into the fray. In the end one old man and Uncle Joe nearly came to fisticuffs, but Jimmy broke it up and hauled Uncle Joe away. I left the diner with Aunt Esther, who was clicking her tongue and shaking her head.

"Joe's getting worse. He was always hot-tempered, but you'd think he'd calm down a bit now that he's getting older. But upon my word, ever since he's had the money George left him he's been quarreling with everyone."

George?" I thought.

"Your Uncle George and your Uncle Joe were as different as night and day," Aunt Esther went on. "George lived in the large front room for years, and you could set your clock by him. Never lost his temper, and always the same schedule, day in and day out. Every morning at six promptly he came out of his room, down the stairs, and out for a walk. If I told him once, I told him a hundred times to hold onto the banister. Those stairs are so steep, you know—but George hated anything that might make him look as though he was getting old. Such a pity, wasn't it?"

"Yes indeed," I murmured, having gathered that George had fallen down the stairs in the early morning and killed himself.

We were the first to reach our compartment, and we settled ourselves comfortably at the two window seats. After a minute or two of silence I asked cautiously, "Who was the woman with red hair who stayed with you last winter?"

"Oh, that one." Aunt Esther laughed a little. "She had the reddest hair I've ever seen on a human head. Very lah-de-dah—you know the sort. Always had a black chiffon veil hanging from her hat—and I don't believe I ever saw her without the hat. She had a room on the second floor, but she didn't have her meals with us. I can tell you, I was glad when she left. She had Eileen fascinated, and the child trailed her around all the time. She was with us for only a week, but when she left I felt it was high time. It was the week George fell down the stairs, you know, and after he died Eileen wanted to go in mourning by wearing a black chiffon veil on her hat."

Mary, Wilfred, and Eileen poured into the compartment just then, and the kid set up a wail because she said one of the window seats was hers—she had left it only to have breakfast, and it wasn't fair. Mary sharply told her to be quiet and to try and behave like a little lady, but I moved over, and, the kid brightened up and slipped in by the window.

"You see," she explained to me, "I'm not as tall as the rest of you, and if I don't have a window seat, I just can't see out at all."

I said, "Uh-huh," and settled my head against the back of the seat. I closed my eyes and tried to relax my mind, and after a while I began to remember faces—vaguely familiar faces—but I could not put a name to any one of them. It was confusing and irritating, and I presently tried concentrating on the Pullman and the elderly woman in the white suit. I began to remember some of the details of that train, even some of the passing scenery, and the elderly woman became clearer—became so clear, in fact, that quite suddenly I knew she was my Aunt Shep. I saw us both as we left the train at Los Angeles. I had no doubt at all about it having been Los Angeles but I could not get beyond that, try as I would. And Aunt Shep was still hardly more than a name to me—I didn't really know her.

I went off to sleep at that point, and I was awakened by the noise of the family stampeding to hurl themselves and their luggage off the train. Jimmy, indolent and unhurried as usual, suggested that he drop Eileen out of the window with the luggage to save time—but he was ignored in the fury of departure. Clive was nowhere to be seen.

Port Pirie Junction was just a place to change trains, and the other train was waiting for us. I bought a newspaper and was troubled when I saw that the date was December eighteenth. I didn't seem to have any Christmas presents for any of these people—certainly there were none in the suitcase which I was sure belonged to the other girl. I glanced over some of the headlines, but they confused me hopelessly.

I folded the newspaper and tucked it under my arm just as Clive appeared at my elbow.

"Better come along—your family are getting on the train. I think they're serving lunch now, so we might as well go along and get some."

"But we've only just had breakfast."

"Can't have it too late, though, or we'll miss our afternoon tea."

"No, no," I said. "Anything but that."

He gave me an oblique glance. "Don't give me any of your lip. Poor Bill loves his afternoon tea."

"Poor Bill," I repeated thoughtfully. "I wonder why Jimmy had to be held off, anyway—he seems quite nice."

"Still suffering from amnesia, I see," Clive said with false courtesy.

"I'm beginning to remember a few things—and no thanks to you or your M.D."

He laughed and boosted me into the train.

It was a comfortable and luxurious train, this Trans-Australian. There were no Pullmans, but it was composed of compartments which slept two, and I discovered that I was bunking in with Aunt Esther. Mary and Eileen had the compartment on one side of us, and Uncle Joe and Wilfred the other. Jimmy was in with a stranger, two doors down, and Clive was in another carriage.

Aunt Esther was busy arranging her things, so I took myself out of her way and went into the corridor. Jimmy was there, looking idly out of the window, with a half-smoked cigarette in his hand.

"It's getting hotter by the minute," I said, and joined him at the window. The scenery was spacious and splendid, and I admired it in silence until a cluster of red flowers swept by, when I let out an exclamation.

Jimmy looked up at me and laughed. "What a girl for red."

"You needn't make cracks at my costume," I sighed. "These are the other girl's clothes—I'm sure of it."

"What are you talking about?" he demanded, suddenly irritable. "It's not your outfit that I mind—it's that red hair you wore last July."

I shook my head. "It wasn't July—it was in the winter. Everybody says it was winter."

He turned and looked full at me. "If this is some new trick, I'm warning you that it won't work. You know that July is winter in Australia for the very simple reason that you spent some time last winter—in July, to be exact—in Perth. It does not get very cold in Perth, or you would not have worn that thin purple silk negligee when you rushed out—before anyone else appeared—just after poor old George fell down the stairs— and snipped off the piece of string you had tied across the top to trip the old boy up. But of course you know all that. What I had actually started to say is that that purple negligee was hardly the right color for your red hair."

Chapter Eight
TO KEEP FROM THINKING

I STEPPED BACK, with my hand pressed against my mouth and my eyes staring. "What are you saying?" I asked in a strangled whisper.

"Oh, come off it, and stop trying to look surprised. I saw you, and you know I saw you. We needn't mention it again—but we will get married."

"Why on earth do you want to marry me?" I asked wildly.

He dropped his cigarette onto the floor and put his toe on it. "We like the same things," he said coolly, "the same sort of life. But the principal reason is that if I were married to you I'd not be so likely to be had up for blackmail. Of course you could introduce me to some of your movie friends, and perhaps I could break in. I might even get to be a star before you do. It would be exhilarating, the kind of life we could lead together—provided we had the money to lead it."

Uncle Joe appeared, and Jimmy stopped talking abruptly, while I hung onto the window ledge for support.

"Come on, all you lot!" Uncle Joe yelled. "Lunch—come on."

I was herded along with the others, while my mind raced in a mad circle of horror and fear. Jimmy had said I was a *murderess!* But that was impossible, quite impossible. And I had murdered for money, which I was now going to have to share with Jimmy. Oh no, never. I was not the redheaded woman.

In the diner I was put at a table with Aunt Esther, Mary, and Eileen. While the others were busy talking I leaned over and said quietly against Eileen's ear, "You know I wasn't that redheaded woman in Perth last winter. Look at me—you know I wasn't."

She regarded me gravely from under her bang and at last said uncertainly, "Well, I don't know. She always wore veils over her face, so you couldn't see it properly, and she had all that red hair. But you have that lucky penny, and she said—"

40

"Yes, I know," I said hastily, `'but I got that by mistake. It—it works out, you see, because as soon as I got it—by accident—she broke her arm."

"Oh, well," said Eileen, "then you're not that lady. I did think you were, too. I thought you'd come over to see what kind of relatives we were before you paid us a proper visit. We might have been the wrong type of people, and then you wouldn't want to be seen with us—you being an actress and all."

"Eileen, child, whatever are you chattering about?" Mary interposed fussily. "Now, what are you going to have to eat?"

Eileen gave her mother a cold glance and fell to studying the menu with raised eyebrows.

I was conscious of a faint, lifting sense of relief. At least Eileen did not recognize my face—I didn't have to be that dreadful woman with the red hair.

I took the mirror from my pocketbook and examined my hair again, but there was no trace of dye even at the ends. It would have to have grown out since July, and that was impossible. But I was plunged into fear again when the thought occurred to me that the red hair could easily have been a wig.

Aunt Esther glanced at me and said, "You look all right, Cleo—eat your lunch."

I put the mirror away and looked out of the window, consciously trying to turn my mind to something else. We would be coming to desert soon—and the three hundred and thirty miles of straight track that Uncle Joe talked about. There was no sign of the desert yet, though, for trees slipped past the window at fairly regular intervals.

I made some comment on the landscape, and Aunt Esther nodded. "We won't reach that straight bit for a while yet. It's called the Nullarbor Plain, and you'll find it quite interesting."

"Why did we have to change trains at Port Pirie Junction?" I asked, not really caring.

"Chynge of track gauge," Mary explained.

"Change, Mother," said Eileen quietly.

Mary's face darkened to magenta, and she said furiously, "I did not say chynge."

"Port Pirie is a nice town, don't you think?" Aunt Esther interposed hastily.

"Town?" I said in some surprise. "But I thought it was just a sort of place to change trains."

"We were at the Junction," Aunt Esther explained. "It's quite a big town—the largest outside the Metropolitan Area in South Australia."

"What is the Metropolitan Area in South Australia?"

"Adelaide," she said, as though I should have known. "But Port Pirie has a population of about twelve thousand."

I murmured, "Golly! Almost three times the size of Sale. It must be a teeming metropolis."

There was a peculiar silence, and I looked up to see that their faces—including even Eileen's—wore tight-lipped, disapproving expressions. I realized that I had been the American abroad again, and I apologized.

"Please forgive me," I said. "I honestly think Australia is a lovely place—and any crack I take at it is purely jealousy."

This cleared the atmosphere at once, and Mary launched into an amiable description of a place called Beaconsfield, in Western Australia, which was her home town.

"It's near Fremantle," she said, "but it's only a small place. I remember when we were children we used to go to school without our shoes and socks."

"Sometimes," Eileen added, "their feet didn't get washed for a week."

This would have started off another family row, except that Clive made his appearance in the diner, accompanied by a blonde who was laughing shrilly. The family stared first at him and then at me, with outrage, pity, and a touch here and there of malice in their faces. The combined effect was so compelling that it lifted me out of my seat and squarely into the path of the approaching pair.

"Clive," I said too loudly, "this is beyond a joke. You can consider our engagement at an end."

Clive colored, and the blonde's mouth dropped open. She got it working promptly, however, and said vigorously, "Why, honey—don't be like that. He just opened my window for me, and I was coming in to lunch and so was he—so we came together. We weren't going to sit together, honest."

"You'll have to, though," I said carelessly. "There's only that table left."

I waved my arm to show her and was dimly conscious that every eye in the diner—both familiar and strange—was upon me. I didn't care, though, as long as I could keep my mind away from the picture of an elderly gentleman tripping over a piece of string tied across the top of a flight of steep stairs.

"Say!" the blonde yelled suddenly. "You're an American. You never got that accent goin' to the village school around here."

"Neither did you. We'll have to get together sometime." I glanced around and saw that Clive had quietly eased himself into my vacated seat. Some of the diners had discreetly lowered their eyes to their plates, while the others, unable to stand the strain, were still staring. Uncle Joe, that valiant soul, had heaved himself out of his chair and was walking into the spotlight to break it up.

" 'Ere, 'ere," he said. "What's all this, eh?"

"Here, here," I said automatically, and blushed to the roots of my hair.

The blonde clicked her tongue. "Your boyfriend's embarrassed," she observed, without troubling to lower her voice. "They embarrass awfully easy over here, don't they?"

"It's all right, Uncle Joe," I said hastily. "We—we're old friends— and we were only kidding." I urged the blonde toward the vacant table and added, "Come on, America—let's stop being so loudmouthed and sit down and have a quiet lunch together. Okay?"

"Swell," said the blonde.

We established ourselves at the table, and Uncle Joe retired. Clive had sunk as low as his backbone would let him, in the seat beside Eileen.

"He *is* embarrassed," I said wonderingly. "I guess I shouldn't have done it."

"Oh, nuts!" said the blonde. "They're always waitin' for us to act vulgar over here, so it seems a shame to disappoint them. We don't go on like this at home. What's your name, hon?"

"I—Cleo. Cleo Ballister. What's yours?"

"Mavis Montague. But I don't mind tellin' you, kid, that if Mama was to hear it, she wouldn't reckernize it. I'm from California—where do you come from?"

"Well—California too."

"You don't say!" She beamed at me. "Let's have a little drink to California."

We did. In fact, we had several little drinks, until at last Mavis decided that we had better quit before we gave California—to say nothing of the United States—a black eye. We had finished lunch by that time, so we got to our feet and rolled out of the diner with what we thought was all the dignity in the world.

Clive and Jimmy were waiting for us just outside, and Mavis indicated them to me with a jerk of her head. "You take the dark one, hon. and I'll have Red. Okay?"

"Swell," I said.

Jimmy caught at my arm and marched me quickly down the corridor. I blinked at him and said, "Surely you're not embarrassed too? A bum like you."

He remained grimly silent until he got me to his compartment, when he pushed me in and shut the door. I noticed, without caring, that the man with whom he shared it was not there.

"*Must* you be a fool?" Jimmy demanded savagely. "You'll give everything away if you carry on like this. You know that drinking loosens the tongue."

"I think that's very odd," I said vaguely. "But then I don't drink—hardly ever. What did you hear me say that was loose?"

"Nothing," he snapped, "but I wasn't listening. However, Joe is very strict in his views about women drinking—you ought to know that. He doesn't approve of it. How would you like it if he decided to change his will and leave everything to Wilfred, or your half to Eileen? He's very fond of Eileen."

"My half?" I said stupidly. "You mean half his money goes to Wilfred and the other half to me?"

Jimmy almost stamped his foot. "You know that perfectly well. You must know that he actually made that will—I believe he wrote and told you so."

"Could be," I murmured. "Listen, Jimmy, I have to go to my compartment and lie down. I need some sleep or something."

He flung the door open, looked up and down the corridor, and then led me out.

"For God's sake, try and be quiet," he whispered. "That was a damned silly way to break your engagement—it sounded completely false. Anyway, now that it's broken, see to it that it stays that way—or you'll find yourself in the hands of the Perth police."

He opened the door of my compartment, urged me in, and closed it after me. Aunt Esther was not there—but Clive was. He stood up as I came in and gave me a rather penetrating look.

"I guess you'd better go," I said, swaying around with the train. "I have to lie down."

"Yes, I know. Better sleep it off." He guided me to the long seat and helped me to stretch out on it. "Tell me," he said after a moment. "Bill's coming to Perth next week, isn't he?"

I said, "Mm," and raised my head while he settled a pillow under it.

"Nice-looking boy, isn't he? Blond, tall, and thin."

"Yes," I agreed, snuggling my head into the pillow.

There was a moment's silence, and then he said slowly, "I'm sorry—I should have believed you when you told me about it. I knew there was something wrong with you just now in the diner." He grinned suddenly and added, "My first amnesia case, and I turn my back on it. Bill is short, heavy, and a violent redhead. He's in Brisbane and doesn't expect another holiday for some time, because he just had one, and spent it more or less in your company."

Chapter Nine
MISSING BROOCH

I HAD A SUDDEN FEELING of relaxation and peace. I needn't be alone with the thing any more—I could share it with someone. And Clive was not the family; somehow I couldn't tell the family— they were too close, too overpowering. But Clive would help me.

I turned my head on the pillow and said urgently, "Don't go away—stay with me. I want to tell you the whole thing. It's—dreadful."

He upended a suitcase, sat on it, and said, "I'm not going."

"Bring your head closer. I—this has to be whispered."

He lowered his head, smiling. "Wouldn't you rather sleep first and tell me about it later?"

"Oh no—no, no—now," I whispered, moving my head restlessly and wondering a little why I felt that it was so urgent.

He nodded. "Righto—get it off your chest. Probably sleep better if you do."

I told him everything, and he listened in absolute silence.

"You see," I said at the end, "my only hope is that I'm the other girl—that they got us mixed somehow. I know the clothes are not mine."

"But the passport?" he suggested.

"There's no passport—only an application for a driver's license."

"What about the photograph?"

"There was no photograph."

"Where is the application?" he asked, and I handed it over. He studied it for some time and at last said slowly, "Well, I suppose it could be you—but I don't think it is. I'm almost certain that you are not twenty-eight or an actress."

"Oh God!" I moaned, "if only I could believe that. The other girl—her name was Virginia Peters."

"How do you know?" he asked, closing the application and glancing up at me.

46

"I think Mrs. Bunton mentioned it."

"It's possible that you remember it yourself, of course," he said, getting up off the suitcase and replacing it. "In any case, your memory seems to be coming back. I think it's been slowed up by the fact that you're on unfamiliar ground here. Anyway, go to sleep now and try not to worry about it. I'll telegraph back and see whether I can find out to what hospital the other girl was taken. In the meantime don't say any thing to anyone—just keep quiet about it all, as you have been doing."

He went out of the compartment, and I relaxed into the pillow and closed my eyes. I felt considerably comforted and much more peaceful. If Clive could establish the fact that I was Virginia Peters, then everything would be all right again. Perhaps he'd have had an answer to his telegram by the time I woke up again.

The train slowed to a stop, and I raised my head and peered out of the window. Port Augusta. After a moment I saw some of the passengers walking on the platform, and I felt satisfied that Clive would have time to do his telegraphing.

It was very hot, and I got up and removed my sweater and skirt. I was more comfortable after that, and I presently went contentedly off to sleep. I felt much better when I woke up. My wristwatch said almost six o'clock, and I stretched and yawned lazily, reflecting that I had been sleeping for over three hours. The train was stopping again, and I saw through the window that it was a place called Pimba. It was for only a few minutes, however, and then we moved on again.

The compartment was cool now—almost chilly—and I realized that it was air-conditioned. I resumed the gray sweater and skirt, thankful that I could put off wearing the dress with the violent print for a while longer.

After I had washed up and tidied my hair I took another look at the application. It wasn't I—I felt as certain as Clive did that it wasn't. Only, of course, that could be wishful thinking. I made a face at the thing and stuffed it back into the red pocketbook.

I went into the corridor, anxious to find Clive and see whether he had been in touch with that other girl. I felt more confident than ever that I was not Cleo Ballister. I never had liked the name Cleo, anyway; I liked Virginia much better.

Out in the corridor I paused at one of the windows and had a look at the passing landscape. Pastoral still—no sign yet of what they called the Nullarbor Plain. I knew that this plain was supposed to have been completely under water at one time, but I could not be sure whether that knowledge was another recaptured memory or whether one of the family had told me about it.

As I moved away from the window I was struck by a more than disturbing thought. If I were the other girl, wouldn't Jimmy know it? Jimmy, who had seen me before—or at least the redheaded woman who he was convinced was I. Certainly she seemed to have gone around swathed in veils, but Jimmy must have seen more of her than the rest of the family had.

I walked slowly down the corridor, and as I came to Jimmy's compartment I saw that the door was open and that he was sitting there alone. I walked in and looked him straight in the eye. "You know something?" I said clearly. "I am not that redheaded woman who was in Perth last winter."

He got quickly to his feet and I saw a fleeting but unmistakable look of horrified doubt pass over his face.

Relief flooded through me, and, encouraged, I went on boldly, "After all, you didn't see much of her, and you can't say definitely that I'm the same person."

He looked at me steadily for a moment and then said, "No. But I can say definitely that Cleo Ballister and the red-haired woman are the same—and since you are Cleo Ballister, it adds up."

"How do you make that out?" I asked warily.

"It's quite simple. My bank sent me to Kalgoorlie at that time, and I followed you. I was on my way when I stopped that night at Esther's. When you left for Sydney, the next day, I was on the same train for Kalgoorlie. After what I had seen you do, I watched you, naturally. You remember you had to stay overnight at Kalgoorlie. I suppose you were so anxious to leave Perth that you did not wait for a train with better connections. Anyway, we arrived at Kalgoorlie late at night. I followed you to the hotel, and you were still swathed in your veils. You signed your name as Cleo Ballister on the hotel register, which, if I may say so, was a rather stupid move. You should have waited until you arrived in Sydney before changing back to your right name."

"Is that all?" I asked quietly.

"No. You left for Sydney the next morning on the Trans-Australian, and shortly after I returned to Carnarvon, I had a letter from Esther. She said they'd had a letter from Cleo—the first in a month—and I laughed. Cleo had returned to Sydney and could start sending letters again. But you're too bold and reckless—it'll trip you up one of these days. For instance, it's like your devil-may-care impudence to come in here and tell me that you were not in Perth last winter. Now, I warn you, I'm losing patience—and you'll have to be quiet and behave yourself. If you don't know what to do, come and ask me—but don't go around talking first and thinking second—because I mean business. Another thing—don't get any ideas about Joe. The other old ass deserved what he got—but Joe's all right—generous and good-natured and always willing to hand out. Besides, he has a bad heart—so leave him alone.

"We'll be married in Perth, after waiting for a week or so to let our romance develop. After that we'll light out."

"Stop and get your breath," I said shortly. "How can you—how can you want to marry one when you believe what you do about me?"

"That's all right," he said easily. "I sent those letters in case it should turn out that I wanted you—and since I've seen you, I know that I do want you. I'm quite satisfied. I think I shall enjoy being married to you."

"What sort of a job do you have in that bank in—Carnarvon, did you say?"

He nodded. "You don't know Carnarvon. It's a small town, and I'm just a helper to my superior—and he's a hayseed."

I backed away from him and slipped out of the door, but he came after me.

"Where are you going now? Why don't you stay with me, and we can yarn about pleasanter things."

"Some other time," I said coldly. "It will be something to look forward to. Right now I want to talk to the family—I guess they're with Uncle Joe somewhere.

"In the lounge car in the back," he said, smiling faintly. "Joe likes company, and the others follow him around—naturally enough. He has all the money, and the heir apparent, Wilfred, and family have to keep him buttered so that he won't change his will. Perhaps you can butter him more smoothly, so that he'll change it anyway—in your favor. Failing that, you'd better pick up all the ready cash you can get out of him—he's always throwing it around."

I had a sudden desperate feeling that if he didn't stop talking, I'd scream—long and loud. I said in a thin, high voice, "You stay here—it will be better if you're not with me."

He nodded, apparently without taking offense, and said, "I'll see you at dinner, then," and turned back into his compartment.

I made my way toward the rear of the train with my mind working feverishly. Jimmy, with his dark and devious mind, made me shudder. But at least I was still not positively identified as Cleo Ballister. I *couldn't* be that woman—a murderess. I couldn't stand it.

I came face to face with Eileen in one of the corridors, and she said tragically, "You missed your tea."

"Yes, I know. It doesn't matter."

I remembered her knowledge of the lucky penny and was conscious of a cold fear that if Jimmy discovered what she knew, he might take some unpleasant steps of his own.

"Eileen," I said hurriedly, "I hope you didn't tell anyone about that lucky penny, did you?"

"Eh?" said the kid. "Oh, you mean that penny you said she lost and then broke her arm and everything. That's an American penny, isn't it? Have you one you could give me?"

"Yes, I'll find you one," I promised. "But don't tell anyone about that other penny, will you?"

"No, if you don't want me to, only—"

"Look," I said desperately, "it—it will bring you, and me too, the worst bad luck in the world if you ever mention it to anyone."

"Will it really?" Her eye gleamed with pleasurable excitement.

"Yes, it will—I mean it."

"Then I won't tell a living soul," she said gravely. "Honor bright."

She went on her way with a new interest in life, and I continued toward the lounge car. The train gave a sudden lurch, and as I reached for the wall to steady myself another memory from the cloudy past opened up in my mind.

Aunt Shep had a lucky penny which she kept in her top bureau drawer. It was in a room—her room—and that was where she lived. Just that one room with a kitchenette which was shut off into a sort of closet. I could see it quite clearly. There must be a bathroom too, of course— only I couldn't remember the bathroom. And the lucky penny was in the top bureau drawer.

I glanced down at my red pocketbook to compare my own—or Cleo Ballister's—lucky penny with the one I remembered, only I couldn't, because it had disappeared.

Chapter Ten
THE PHANTOM BARK

THE BROOCH HAD BEEN PINNED to a narrow band of silk trimming on the pocketbook, and the silk was ripped and torn. The penny hadn't just fallen off, then—someone had wrenched it off. I thought back to when I had last seen it, and I was pretty certain that it had been when we were at Port Augusta. That meant that while I was sleeping someone had come in and taken it without waking me.

I considered it while the goose pimples rose on my skin. Jimmy? But I did not think, somehow, that he knew anything about it. Eileen! I turned around and flew after her and managed to catch her just as she was entering her compartment.

She denied it, though, so earnestly and shrilly that I felt convinced she was telling the truth. She seemed very much upset about it, in fact, and I had to calm her with promises of a thorough search.

I made for the lounge car again, anxious to find Clive and discover whether he had any news for me.

The car was crowded. There was a piano at one side, and Uncle Joe sat before it, pounding happily while a group of people in the background sang lustily. Clive stood a little apart with Mavis Montague.

She saw me and waved her drink in cheerful greeting. "Hello, hon!" she yelled.

I joined them and asked, "Do you mind if I have a word in private with my ex-fancy?"

"You go right ahead, dearie. I'll order you a little drink in the meantime."

Clive took my arm and we moved away. "I telephoned," he said quietly. "The guard knew of a nursing home around that area where she might have been taken, so I chanced it and got through to them. She'd been there, all right."

"She— You mean she isn't there now?"

He shook his head rather gravely at my eagerness and warned, "It isn't very satisfactory."

"But—"

"Her arm wasn't broken. She'd twisted it a bit, and they strapped it up for her. She stayed through the night but insisted on leaving early the next morning."

"What name did she give?" I asked, blinking back tears of disappointment.

"They had her recorded as Virginia Peters— but the train people might have given them that name. She might not have known about it."

"She must have," I said soberly. "She could not have been unconscious for long, and I suppose she knew what she was doing when she left the next morning."

"She might have been drunk," Clive suggested. "And in that case she might not have noticed about the name—or cared if she did."

I shook my head, feeling dissatisfied, but before we could discuss it any further we were surrounded by Mavis, Aunt Esther, Mary, and Wilfred. Uncle Joe, at the piano, finished with great gusto a selection that seemed to concern somebody waltzing with Matilda. He swung around on the stool, caught sight of me, and joined us.

"Well, you *did* have a sleep, didn't you?" he said affectionately. His eye fell on Mavis, and the walrus mustache bristled with sudden hostility. Obviously Mavis had no standing in the family circle.

She caught the look and responded immediately. "Cleo, honey, introduce me to your uncle."

I nodded and murmured conventionally, thinking wryly that the name Cleo had become almost unbearable to me.

Uncle Joe bowed formally, while his eye remained cold, but Mavis was easily a match for him. She dribbled a few honeyed words into his ear, smiled wistfully, and finally marched him off with her arm tucked in his, to a couple of isolated seats at the rear of the car.

I took a quick look at the faces of Aunt Esther, Mary, and Wilfred, and saw a single emotion stamped on them all. Fear. It was natural, of course, that they should want to keep Uncle Joe single and his money intact for themselves. Not that it would have bothered Cleo to see Mavis walk him off to a corner—Cleo would simply arrange to have Uncle Joe pass on before he could marry Mavis or anyone else. Perhaps she was planning to do away with him in any case, instead of depending on his generosity until he died. It would be simpler than watching constantly to see that he did not marry. Jimmy was sticking his neck out too—the egotistical fool—thinking he could dominate a ruthless character like Cleo. What sort of a life did he expect to have, married to a woman whose whim might lead her to put ground glass in his salad at any time? But with Jimmy it was the movie contracts, of course—and the where-withal to get to Hollywood and make them.

I could quite easily be this Cleo, too. The family had accepted me without hesitation or suspicion. My face and neck came out in a cold, clammy perspiration, and I took my handkerchief and mopped at it with a shaking hand.

Aunt Esther gave me a sharp look and said, "You don't look too well at all, Cleo. Do go back and lie down. I'll have your dinner sent in."

"Oh no—no. I'm all right. When do we go to dinner?"

Wilfred pulled out his watch. "We're waiting for Uncle Joe now," he said, frowning.

"Oh," I laughed, "if that's all, I'll get him for you right away. Mavis is only trying to get a mink coat out of him, and she can continue after dinner just as well."

Mary moaned, "What!" and looked ready to faint. Clive said, "I'll get him. You people go on ahead and collect Jimmy and Eileen."

They started off, glancing back over their shoulders uneasily until we had left the car.

Mary drew a long breath of recovery, blew her nose, and sensibly turned her mind to other things.

"I do hope you won't think me too inquisitive," she said tentatively, "but have you actually broken your engagement with Clive?"

"Oh no. That was just horseplay."

"I see—well, that's a good thing. Is that Mavis really an old friend of yours, as you told Uncle Joe in the diner?"

"No," I said. "I was just smoothing things over."

"I shouldn't let Clive have too much to do with her if I were you," Aunt Esther warned.

"Oh well, that's up to him," I replied carelessly. "If he decides to take her on and throw me over, there are plenty of fish left in the sea. Bigger ones, maybe."

They didn't laugh. Mary compressed her lips and frowned, and Wilfred gave me a look that suggested admiration at my fortitude in hiding my breaking heart. He said dourly, "There should be some legal way of dealing with hussies like that girl."

"Oh no," I protested. "Mavis is quite fair and open about it all. She doesn't conceal any of her weapons."

Mary said grimly, "Indeed she doesn't," and then suddenly went off into peals of laughter, while Wilfred looked shocked.

"Tell me," I said after a while, "do I look much like the photos you have of me?" The thought had occurred to me that they would probably have photographs, and I asked the question almost fearfully.

"No, you don't," Aunt Esther said promptly. "But we've only those few snapshots. You're doing your hair differently, aren't you?"

I said "Yes" and felt relief flowing through me again.

The train stopped, and we swarmed to the windows and looked out.

"Wirraminna," Wilfred said, squinting into the late sunlight.

"Do we change our watches here?" Mary asked.

"No, no—that comes much later. I'll tell you when."

We collected Eileen and Jimmy and wended our way to the diner. We found two tables for four opposite each other, and Aunt Esther directed the seating arrangements.

"You go there," she said to me, "with your young gentleman, and Joe and Wilfred. Mary, you and Eileen sit here with me—and Jimmy."

Eileen and Jimmy objected promptly. Jimmy wanted to sit with me, and Eileen was determined to sit with Uncle Joe—so that by the time Clive appeared with Mavis and Uncle Joe, we were still milling around.

Mavis promptly eased into one of our tables and pulled Uncle Joe down beside her, while Aunt Esther remained standing in the aisle, completely nonplused. Jimmy pushed me in opposite Mavis and was about to seat himself beside me when Uncle Joe put a stop to it.

" 'Ere, now, you let Cleo's young man sit beside her."

Jimmy backed away to the other table, and Clive sat down. Wilfred pulled out a chair for his mother, but she remained standing and cried shrilly, "Eileen! Where are we going to put Eileen? There isn't room for five here, Joe. What are we going to do?"

Uncle Joe blew through his walrus and said calmly, "Esther, my girl, sit you three at one table and two at another—and save your fuss for when it's needed."

Aunt Esther frowned and turned away. She curtly ordered Jimmy and Wilfred to a table for two and seated herself at last with Mary and Eileen.

It immediately developed that Uncle Joe was in a good mood. He flung quips right and left, and Mavis roared with laughter and winked at me in between times. Once she gave him a hearty push on the shoulder and broke one of her long red fingernails. She stopped laughing to grieve over the damage and sighed, "Now wouldn't that slay you? And no manicure things with me."

"Cheer up," Uncle Joe said without sympathy. "I like hands that haven't been mucked up with red paint, anyway."

She grinned reluctantly, but her eyes still mourned. "Listen, big boy, if I don't have my nail polish and lipstick on, I feel downright nood."

Things were lively again for a while, and then Mavis, reaching for the salt, dipped her sleeve into her plate of soup.

"Oh, damn it to hell!" she said furiously.

Uncle Joe, who had been halfway through a lively anecdote, stopped dead and looked at her in shocked surprise. When he could speak at all he said reprovingly, "Now, that's not a nice way to talk, little lady."

He was quiet after that, and though Mavis, Clive, and I chatted to keep things going, he had very little to say. Aunt Esther presently called him to ask if he had taken his pill, and he snapped at her irritably.

"I'm not a ruddy imbecile—I know I have to take my pill."

He fumbled into his pockets and brought out a small box wrapped in paper. He tore off the wrapping impatiently, opened the box, and stared at the contents with bulging eyes.

"Look at that;" he stammered. "Look what that fool of a chemist in Melbourne has done."

Aunt Esther leaned across the aisle and surveyed the box of small gumdrops that he held out to her. "Jujubes," she said. "Really, Joe, you're getting more absent-minded every day."

"Whaddya mean, absent-minded?" Uncle Joe roared. "What about the chemist being absent-minded? He did this, not me."

Aunt Esther shook her head more in sorrow than anger, and Mary said thoughtlessly, "But the *chemist* would hardly make a mistake like that."

Uncle Joe promptly gave her a severe scolding, and Aunt Esther came in for some of it too—although she did nothing but continue to shake her head at intervals.

I was developing a headache and mentioned it more to make conversation than for any other reason, but Aunt Esther pounced on me at once. I must go along to our compartment and get the bottle of aspirins which she had wedged in behind the water. carafe. Now, at once, before my head got any worse.

"You do like she says, hoe," Mavis said seriously. "You don't wanna let that headache get the best of you. Why, I've had headaches in any time that were fit to knock my hat right off."

I went along to the compartment and found the aspirins readily enough. I took two, washed them down with water, and then dropped onto the seat and looked out of the window.

It was eight o'clock new and getting dark, and there was not much to see. I was in the middle of a yawn, when right beside me, as it seemed, a dog barked.

I sprang to my feet and looked around the narrow, compact little room—and there was no dog.

Chapter Eleven
THE MOLE

I BACKED TO THE DOOR of the compartment and nearly fell out into the corridor. I stood there for a while, nervously telling myself that the dog must have been in the next compartment—and then I heard it again. It was not very loud, the bark of a small dog rather than a large one, and it came quite unmistakably from my own compartment

I turned and fled back to the dining-car. I had intended to tell the family and bring them back to investigate, but when I got there I found that I couldn't. I had an uneasy feeling that they'd think I was crazy—I felt a bit crazy, anyway. I knew that Clive was watching me and that he had sensed something wrong. He waited until Mavis and Uncle Joe, who seemed to have cheered up, had gone into a noisy burst of laughter, and then leaned toward me and asked quietly, "What's the matter?"

"There's a dog barking in my compartment—only there isn't any dog there."

He looked so astonished that I added forlornly, "I guess I'm going crazy."

He thought it over for a moment, frowning at his cigarette, and then said abruptly, "Let's go and investigate."

I nodded. "Only wait till I finish my coffee."

"What are you two cookin' up?" Mavis asked. "What are you goin' to do when you finish the Java?"

Clive, relaxed back into his chair and abstractedly fingering his coffee spoon, looked up at her and said lazily, "Nothing exciting. Just a game of drafts."

"Drafts?" said Mavis. "What's that? Anyhow, I don't wanna play. I wanna dance and drink."

"Quite all right," Clive agreed amiably. "We need only two for drafts."

Jimmy loomed up beside me and said, "Cleo, let's go to the lounge car and have coffee there."

"I'm having it here," I said mildly, "and I'm halfway through. Then I have to play a game of drafts with Clive—but after that we can have a smoke together, if you like."

"Drafts!" Jimmy muttered, astounded. "I thought even the kids stopped playing it. Well, play if you must—but bear in mind that I'm a jealous type. You break your engagement with old sawbones here—become engaged to me—and I can't even get hold of you for a cup of coffee."

There was a combined gasp from the family, and Mavis said to me with genuine admiration, "Gee, kid, are you a fast worker!"

I stood up quickly and said, "Your joke's in bad taste, Jimmy." For the benefit of the family I added, "He's only trying to be funny. Come on, Clive, let's have that game of drafts—only you'll have to teach me how to play, because I've never even heard of it. See you later, Jimmy."

Mavis demanded, in a voice that carried to the far corners of tile diner, "How does she get that way? All the fellas chasin' her. What's the matter with me?"

Eileen's thin, precise treble explained it to her. "Cleo's an heiress, you see."

There was an astounded silence that shaped itself into keen embarrassment. I made my escape without so much as a glance over my shoulder, but I heard Eileen being scolded by Mary, who sounded shocked to breathlessness.

Clive had followed close behind me, and as soon as we were clear of the diner he said urgently, "We'll go along to your compartment. We're rid of friend Jimmy for the moment, hut he'll be back before we get lonesome for him. The fellow's like sticking plaster."

Back in my compartment, we stood around with our ears quivering, but of course the invisible dog refused to bark. I gave Clive a despairing look, and he pulled me down onto the seat. "Forget about the dog and try to relax. You're working up to the tension of a violin string."

I sighed and presently told him about the conversation I had had with Jimmy. He became very grave indeed over that, and when I had finished he said grimly, "This is pretty bad. But there's a mistake somewhere, of course—there has to be."

"If I could just talk to that other girl," I whispered miserably, "I'm sure it would all come right."

"Don't worry too much about it. I've put a firm of detectives on her trail, and they ought to turn her up shortly. Now, about this memory of yours—has there been anything more?"

"Yes," I said. "Aunt Shep saw me off on the boat—and I was coming here."

He questioned me eagerly about that, but I could not tell him any more—I could not supply any details. It was like a blurred picture that would not focus. I tried very hard, but we had to give up at last.

"About Jimmy," Clive said. "Don't give in to him, but parry him along until you can get some more information."

"All right," I agreed wearily, "I'll do the best I can. But let's go and have our game of drafts. I want to think about something else just for a little while."

"Good," he said, and stood up. "I'll teach you how to play. My father taught me—he was the champion of Sale."

We left the compartment and headed toward the lounge car. It was quite dark outside now, and when I looked out of the window I could see nothing but the reflection of the lights inside.

"You'll be able to see when the moon comes up," Clive said. "It's very bright."

"Have you made this trip before?" I asked curiously.

"Oh yes. I've a married sister in Perth, and since the death of my father my mother lives with her."

"Hmm," I said. "I was wondering why you were traveling away from Sale instead of toward it."

"I'd like to settle down in Sale, though," he declared earnestly.

"Nothing doing. I don't like small towns."

I heard him give an odd little cough behind me, and I realized what I had said. I stopped walking and turned around, and I could feel my face glowing a bright red,

"You see?" I said desperately. "That proves it—I *am* crazy. First I hear dogs barking when there aren't any, and then—well, you'll have to excuse me."

He laughed easily. "Don't let it upset you. I can't explain the dog, but this other is just a wish to belong to somebody—to attach yourself, because I don't think you really believe these others are your relatives."

"All right," I broke in hastily "let it go at that. I realize that you probably have a sweetheart in Sale or Perth. Sale, probably—nice small-town girl—has your wholehearted approval."

"What about a wife?" he asked, and sounded amused.

"Well, you—you're a rat for taking on this assignment if you have a wife."

He laughed again. "You city slickers are just the same as the small-town girls. You all want to know whether a chap's married or has a sweetheart."

"My, my," I said, "and you're going to play coy and not tell me."

We went along to the lounge car, and Clive produced an ordinary checkerboard. He pulled two chairs up to a small table, and as I sat down. I thought, without any effort at all, of my father. He had taught *me* how to play checkers, too. But he was dead. I did not know when or how he had died—but he was dead.

Clive looked up at me and asked, "What is it?"

"My father," I said dully. "He—he's dead. If he were alive, I could get in touch with him—"

Clive shook his head. "Not if you can't remember any more about him than you do about your Aunt Shep."

I looked down at the checkers. I knew the game very well—in fact, I was good at it. My father's name had not been Ballister, either. Only I could not get a glimmer of any other name, so how could I be sure that Ballister was wrong?

"If your memory hasn't cleared by the time we get to Perth," Clive said, "we'll get to work on it. But I think you'll find it will be back before then. In the meantime stop bothering about things, and I'll tell you how to play this game."

"Don't bother," I said modestly. "I know the rules."

I beat him quite easily, and he was a bit taken aback, but he suggested another game, with plenty of confidence to spare. I found the second game easier to win than the first, and Clive's face was a mixture of amazement and chagrin. Also, a small crowd of people had collected around us.

"We'll have try more game," Clive said, exhibiting the old fighting spirit. "I always thought I was pretty good."

I made a face at him. "Population four thousand five hundred," I jeered. "You've never had any competition. If you have a talent, it's had no opportunity to develop. At least I know that I'm nobody in the checker world, but you're easy—I can beat you any time."

Clive gritted his teeth and muttered, "Ten shillings this time."

A bookie appeared like magic from out of the crowd, and bets were taken to the satisfaction of all. I rerolled the sleeves of my sweater, and we started in.

This time it was not so easy—in fact, it was so difficult that I lost. I was tired by that time, but the crowd was so eager that I played two more games. I split those, which left me ten shillings to the bad, but Uncle Joe paid that cheerfully. He had bet only on the game I won and was feeling pretty good.

I noticed that Jimmy was over in a corner with Mavis. They had drinks and were chatting with a certain amount of animation. Aunt Esther was reading a magazine, and Mary had disappeared, presumably engaged in the serious and complicated business of putting Eileen to bed. The checker game was still booming, someone else having taken my seat opposite Clive, with the Australian gambling spirit in full swing.

Wilfred apparently didn't gamble, for he was wandering around aimlessly, until he presently drifted over to me and began to talk. I let him ramble on, but I didn't listen much, although I heard bits here and there. He and Mary would have liked a boy, as well as Eileen, but the Lord wouldn't or couldn't provide. Also, he worked very hard in his garden of a Sunday.

I swallowed a yawn and thought longingly of my bed. It was nearly ten o'clock, and through a crack of one of the blinds I could see that the moon was coming up. I hated to admit it, even to myself, but I was afraid to go to the compartment alone, because of the dog that barked and yet remained invisible. I'd wait for Aunt Esther, I decided, and go along with her, when she went. I didn't think that she'd be very late.

I turned back to Wilfred and was faintly surprised to discover that he was no longer beside me. I felt a moment's spasm of remorse and hoped I hadn't been too rude to him.

Mavis pushed her way through the crowd and joined me, and I saw that Jimmy was now deep in the checker gamble. She looked me over, patted her blond locks, and said elegantly, "My dear! I never connected the name before. You're that actress, aren't you? Why, I've seen you in the movies, and I think you're wonderful. I always notice that cute little mole you have on your chin. Some of the dopes would cover that mole up—but you never do, and you're smart. It's cute as hell."

Chapter Twelve
LOST LIZARD

"WELL," I THOUGHT, with the calmness of utter despair, "that seems to prove it." I did not need to take out the little mirror and look at my chin—I knew that the mole was there, only it was more like a big freckle than anything else.

So I was Cleo Ballister. I swallowed something that seemed to be choking me and raised my chin. I had not killed my uncle, anyway—no matter what Jimmy said and despite the lucky penny. Where was the penny, for that matter? There must have been a reason for someone creeping in and tearing it off my pocketbook. Eileen seemed the most likely person, but she had showed concern over its loss and was searching for it. That might all have been put on, of course, to hide the feet that she had stolen it.

I came back to my surroundings to realize that Jimmy had wandered up and was looking at me crossly, and Mavis seemed a bit offended because I had not answered her.

"I'm sorry," I said inadequately. "There's so much noise here—it's confusing."

"Terrible," Mavis agreed, cheerful once more. "A girl don't know if she's coming or going. Say, I tell you what—let's get off at Tarcoola and have a quick snack before we go to bed."

"Tarcoola?"

"It's our next stop," Jimmy explained. "But there won't be time for a snack—we can have something to eat here on the train. Our watches go back forty-five minutes between Tarcoola and Barton."

The train slowed down and stopped as he spoke, and Mavis jumped to her feet. "Come on, we'll get a hunk of fresh air, anyways."

It was queer, almost ghostly, out on that station. The air was hot and very still, and the moon and hundreds of stars gave a silver light that was disturbing in its brilliance.

62

Uncle Joe came looking for us after a while and hustled us back onto the train.

"You shouldn't do things like that," he said severely. "You might get left behind. Come on now —I've got sandwiches for us, and then we all ought to go to bed."

Jimmy looked rebellious but held his peace, and we all followed Uncle Joe meekly back into the train, where we found Aunt Esther, Mary, Wilfred, and Clive all more or less grouped around a plate of sandwiches.

"Tuck in, everybody," Uncle Joe commanded, "and then we'll go to bed. It's getting late."

"I'm going to have a look at the Nullarbor Plain," Clive said, biting into a sandwich. "It's due in about half an hour."

Jimmy lit a cigarette and leaned back in his chair with a superior look on his face. "It's nothing—only a bunch of ghostly looking bushes in the moonlight."

" 'Ow do you know?" Uncle Joe asked repressively. "You only saw it in the daytime."

"How," said Aunt Esther.

"I read about it," Jimmy said shortly.

Mavis reached politely for the last sandwich. "I'll stay up with you."

Clive shook his head. "I'm going to watch from my own compartment, and the man who lives with me might want to go to bed."

"My," I said.

Clive looked up at me. "Beg pardon?"

"Nothing. Only I don't see why you can't sit out here and watch, and Mavis can sit with you. I'm going to bed myself. I can always read about it—like Jimmy."

"Joe, you're going to bed, aren't you?" Aunt Esther asked. "I hope you haven't any idea of sitting up and painting all night."

Uncle Joe blew thoughtfully through his walrus and considered it. "Well, now, I don't know. I really should set up my things near the ones who are going to watch, and then they can tell me their impressions and I'll paint them down."

"Paint down *impressions?*" Mary bleated.

"You ask any real painter, my girl," Uncle Joe said belligerently. "When anybody describes things to me I can see it all vividly—and I can paint it down, too."

Aunt Esther stood up and smoothed her dress over her hips. "Perhaps you can, Joe, but your health should come first. You come along now and go to bed, and you can get up very early in the morning. I like a sunrise better than a moonlight landscape, anyway."

Joe nodded and heaved himself to his feet. "Righto. I'll get up at four, and then I'll catch the sun no matter how early it rises. Come on, Wilfred—you come along with me. I don't want you disturbing me by clattering in later."

Wilfred stood up and said mousily, "Yes, yes—I was just coming anyway."

Aunt Esther and Mary began to move away, and then Aunt Esther paused and said to me, "Stay as long as you want to, Cleo—you won't disturb me when you come in. I sleep like a log."

I smiled at her. "Thanks. I'll be along soon. Good night."

A chorus of good nights flew back and forth until they had all gone, and Mavis, Clive, Jimmy, and I were left to ourselves.

Clive told us to put our watches back. "We're due in at Barton at midnight, and that's on Central time."

" 'Something, oh something Time, in thy flight,' " Mavis trilled. "Who cares about time? Let's all have a drink."

"I doubt it," Clive said. "Not at this time."

"Yes, we can." Jimmy got to his feet. "If you'll step along to my compartment, I have a bottle of the best. Nor will my roommate interfere with us, because I see him sitting over there in a corner, reading."

Mavis received this invitation with gusty enthusiasm, and when I murmured a preference for my bed, she and the other two firmly overruled me. I gave in at last, thinking that perhaps a drink or two might take my mind off the wretched freckle on my chin. I knew I should tell Clive about the freckle, and knew, too, that I didn't want to. He wouldn't like me much if I were Cleo—I wouldn't like myself.

I had tried to bring Aunt Shep back into my mind, to see if it would revive any instance of her calling me Cleo. If I could remember that she had ever called me Cleo—just once—I'd be convinced. But somehow, when I brought her to my mind, I almost unconsciously brushed her out again—and I knew that it was because I was afraid. She had seen me off on the boat and had waved to me from the pier. At the last moment she had called out to me—and I was afraid to remember what she had said. It could so easily have been, "Good-by, Cleo."

We had settled ourselves in Jimmy's compartment, and he gave me a calculating look.

"What are you thinking about?"

"Nothing," I said shortly. "I'm tired. I'll have one drink, and then I'm going to bed."

"Oh, don't be such a droop!" Mavis yelled, slapping me on the back. "Come on—bottoms up!"

Jimmy disposed of his drink rather quickly and then turned to Clive with one eyebrow elevated. "Look here, you don't really mind if I cut you out with Cleo? I know the whole thing is only tomfoolery—it's quite evident to everybody but Joe—and he's a bit dense, anyway."

"Nah, he doesn't mind," Mavis observed, reaching for the bottle.

"Yes, I do," Clive said equably. "I'm young and at the beginning of my career, and I understand Cleo is coming into some money."

Jimmy sat back and laughed. "That's what I mean, you see—tom-foolery. Be reasonable, and let's switch over this engagement tonight."

"Money," said Mavis almost sadly, "certainly talks awful loud. How do you guys know I'm poor, anyway?"

Clive, sitting forward with his arms resting on his knees, slowly turned his glass between his two hands. "What about Cleo?" he asked without looking up. "How does she feel?"

"Don't bring me into it," I said hastily. "Settle it between yourselves. Maybe you can think of some way to divide the money."

Jimmy's hand closed almost viciously around my arm, and Mavis, starting a guffaw, choked on her drink and seemed about to strangle. Clive gave her a few vigorous slaps on the back, and in the ensuing uproar Jimmy said against my ear, "You watch yourself and play up to me. I'm serious."

I looked him over coldly. "I'm not sure that I wouldn't rather be in the hands of the Perth police."

He shrugged and muttered, "Suit yourself," but his eyes were dark with anger.

Mavis, somewhat recovered and mopping at her streaming eyes, told an involved tale of how a man had choked to death just that way. Clive had started to top it with the story of a man in Sale who had got a fishbone stuck in his throat, when Jimmy's roommate walked into the compartment. He looked us over stonily, and Jimmy offered him a drink. It appeared, however, that he never drank, and that if we didn't mind, he'd like to get to bed.

"But we do mind," Mavis said frankly. "Here we are, having a swell party, and you walk your ugly puss in here and want to break it up."

"That's a pity," said the man, putting it mildly. "But I paid for this berth, and I intend to use it."

Mavis told him to go ahead and hit the hay and not bother about us, because we were broad-minded—but the rest of us hustled her out, still arguing shrilly.

The train had stopped, and Jimmy looked out one of the corridor windows. "We're at Barton. Let's go out and look at the stars."

We went out and walked slowly up and down, breathing the warm, still air. I was amazed and thrilled again at the extraordinary brilliance of the moon and stars. It was almost frightening.

After we had returned to the train we decided to go to bed, and Clive and Mavis went off in one direction while Jimmy and I went back to our own car. Jimmy accompanied me to the door of my compartment, and before I realized his intention he had kissed me good night. It was not a diffident or cousinly kiss, either, and it made me angry.

"You are not to do that ever again," I said quietly. "Not unless eve are officially engaged—if we ever are."

"Is there any doubt about it in your mind?" he asked, narrowing his eyes at me.

I turned my back on him and went into the compartment.

Aunt Esther had pulled up the shade, and the small room was filled eerily with silver moonlight. I could see everything quite clearly, except Aunt Esther's head, which was in the shadow. I supposed she was asleep, since she did not stir, and I went quietly to the window and sat down.

The plain—we must be on it now. There were still a few trees, but they were small and stunted, and everywhere was the bush—saltbush and bluebush. I rested my forehead against the pane, and as I sat there the trees were finally left behind and there was only the bush. Clumps of grayish green and bluish white—ghost bushes in the moonlight.

I thought of being out on that plain all alone and felt a chill creeping along my spine.

There was a knock on the door, and I started and then hurried to open it. Wilfred stood in the corridor, his wispy hair rumpled and a shabby robe belted untidily around him.

He blinked at me and said, "Oh—sorry to wake you up. Will you wake Mother? Uncle Joe is pretty bad—and beside that, he's lost his lizard."

Chapter Thirteen
BLOODY TRACKS

"UNCLE JOE HAS LOST a *lizard?*" I asked feebly.

"Yes, yes." Wilfred edged into the compartment. "Mother! Mother, do wake up."

Aunt Esther stirred and turned over. "What is it?"

Wilfred repeated his peculiar news, and she got out of bed and pulled on a wrapper. She seemed cross, rather than alarmed. "Joe always thinks he can eat or drink anything," she said, and bustled out after Wilfred. I was left alone, wondering foolishly whether she meant that Joe had eaten his lizard.

I went and sat by the window, hugging my arms close around me and trying to think of a lizard running suddenly up the wall and dropping onto my neck or shoulder. I looked out at the still, silent moonlit bush and was vaguely reminded of a cemetery. All those dead bushes, I thought idiotically, walking the plain and returning to their graves in the morning. I tried to shake my mind free from such nonsense and to remember, sensibly, that the bush would still be there tomorrow, under the sunlight. Probably, I thought bitterly, if I were not so distracted about a freckle on my chin, just to mention one of my troubles, I would find the moonlit bush peaceful and beautiful.

I rested my cheek and forehead against the pane. It was not like ordinary train riding, this—we seemed almost to be floating through endless acres of moonlight and saltbush. I had a strong impression that the train had slowed down, but I knew that it had not. I had been told that it always seemed that way on an absolutely straight track, and this straight track lasted for three hundred and thirty miles. The sensation of floating through a spectral company of watching, silvered bushes became so hypnotic that I turned away from the window at last, shaking my head confusedly, to try and clear away the impression.

I had better go to bed, I thought. I could lie there, relaxed, and perhaps some more memories would come back to me. I must not hold them off because I was afraid—I must find out who I was and who Aunt Shep was, and all about myself. I was terrified, though, and I knew it. Terrified that I was Cleo, the heiress who certainly would not bother waiting too long to get her hands on the money.

I did not trouble to pull the shade and put on the light, but with my sweater pulled half over my head I wondered suddenly whether I ought to go and see how Uncle Joe was. They might need help. Probably they didn't, though—I might be in the way. Aunt Esther was competent, and she had Wilfred to help her.

I pulled the sweater back on and stood there for a moment, undecided. And then the little dog barked again—right beside me.

I gasped and flew out into the lighted corridor, where I leaned against the wall and tried to get my breath. What was the matter with me, anyway? There was no dog in that compartment, and Uncle Joe on one side and Mary and Eileen on the other had no dogs with them, either. Anyway, I was certain that the sound was in my own room. It did not seem exactly like a real dog, I thought uneasily—more like the ghost of one, like those bushes floating by outside.

I put my hands to my head and tried to stop my whirling thoughts, and after a moment, when I was breathing more quietly, I went over to Uncle Joe's door and knocked. Wilfred stuck his head out, and I asked, "Is there anything I can do to help?

"No, no, thanks very much. He's a bit easier now. Mother always knows what to do for him when he gets these attacks of indigestion."

"Did he find his lizard?"

"No—no, he didn't. He was painting it over again, you know—swears someone else finished that other painting—but I don't know who could have done it."

I stood and blinked at him, feeling thoroughly confused.

"I wonder," said Wilfred diffidently, "whether you'd care to go along to the lounge car and have a look. I know he took it out there today, and he might have lost it there. It's bothering him, and we'd like to find it for him and set his mind at rest."

"Of course," I agreed. "I'll go at once."

I started off toward the lounge car, still a little confused but having gathered that Uncle Joe's lizard was merely the painting I had seen and not a live creature. He was doing the painting over again because he had not liked the first attempt—and neither had I for that matter. It was terrible. It seemed odd, though, that he had tried to cover up by saying that someone else had spoiled it. I thought of the box of gumdrops which he had thought were pills and wondered whether he was a bit queer—or maybe someone was trying to make him appear as though he were going crazy. Perhaps someone *had* painted that picture over—and substituted the gumdrops for his pills. The thought struck me so hard that I stopped walking to recover from it. I knew I wasn't doing it, and yet it was exactly the sort of thing that Cleo would think up. Have Uncle Joe safely tucked away in an asylum and then get control of his money. Maybe Aunt Esther was doing it. She hated the way he was throwing his money around—her dear little Wilfred's money.

"Oh, shut up!" I said aloud, and went on to the lounge car.

I was far from pleased to find Jimmy there, sitting in an armchair and staring at the ground. He raised his head and said, "Oh, hello. Looking for me?"

"You might do, I should think. I'm looking for a lizard."

"You keep a civil tongue in your head," he said, but without venom. "It's Joe, is it?"

I nodded and began to search through a pile of magazines and books. He watched me for a while in silence and assumed a faint amused smile. "Do you expect to find the poor thing flattened out between two books? I don't think Joe would have any use for the dead body."

"But—am I supposed to be looking for a live lizard?"

"It was alive the last I heard," he said indifferently.

"It's a painting," I told him. "I saw it myself. A lizard on some green grass."

"I've no doubt—but that's not what you're looking for. Joe would be only too happy to lose a painting—give him an immediate excuse to do another. But the fact that he had lost his model would break his heart."

I dropped into a chair and said, "Give me a cigarette."

He handed over something with a fancy basketweave tip, but it smoked all right.

"You know," he said presently, "you're all right, really. Your past is pretty bad, but I think, with me, you can overcome that. I know that money makes people do terrible things at times—but we could forget all about it and simply look to the future. Let's hurry the thing along and get away."

Jimmy trying to make himself sound all right to himself. Cleo's murder was to be forgotten, and she was not to do another. I sighed over his self-confident idiocy and said, "I didn't do any of that, you know—I honestly didn't. There's been some sort of a mistake—"

"All right—I know," he broke in quickly. "We'll just forget it."

"Making up to my affianced again, I see," Clive observed from the doorway.

We both jumped, and Jimmy said irritably, "I thought you were going to view the scenery from your own compartment."

"So I was—but the old boy who bunks in with me objected. Said he had to have the shade drawn because the bluebush made him nervous. Seems the saltbush doesn't bother him at all, but the bluebush reminds him of a past sorrow."

Jimmy put out his cigarette and got to his feet. "I won't do battle with you face to face," he said negligently. "Only remember this—if she is not affianced to me now, she will be before this journey is over."

He took himself off, and Clive sat down and grinned at me. "Is he bothering you too much?"

I shook my head, thinking that I felt a little sorry for Jimmy. He wanted so badly to be a big town boy, but he couldn't make it by himself—he had to have someone to give him a boost.

I told Clive about the freckle on my chin, and to my deep disappointment he said nothing, but stared thoughtfully in front of him. I had been hoping against hope that he would somehow explain away the freckle.

I watched him anxiously, and he presently turned to me and said, "Your memory is clearing slowly—but I think you're holding back on it."

"Yes, I know—I realize that. It's because I'm afraid."

"But that won't help you," he said. "You must try to relax and let it come."

"I'll try—but not here—not now." I moved my head restlessly and looked at the one dim light that had been left burning in the car. "I'm supposed to be looking for a lizard—a live one."

He looked so astounded that I explained hastily and then went on to tell him of my suspicion that someone was trying to railroad Uncle Joe into the asylum.

Clive would have none of it. "Your imagination is getting the best of you—come down to earth. Joe's all right, and so are his relatives— decent, sober people. The old man is absent-minded and stubborn, and since he holds the family purse, he expects them to sit up and agree when he makes a statement."

"Are you sober and decent too?" I asked idly.

It took him a moment to come off the soapbox, and then he laughed.

"I was brought up on Macalister Street in Sale—which answers your question, whether you realize it or not."

"Such elegance," I sighed. "And for all I know, I may have been dragged up in the slums of Park Avenue, New York."

"Don't be too humble," he said kindly. "We can't all be born to the purple, and in this day and age there is always opportunity for the underdog."

I moved over to one of the windows and pulled the shade aside. I could almost have sworn now that we had slowed down, although the bush still floated lazily by. I shivered and turned away. "I believe I could enjoy this," I said querulously, "if only my mind were at rest."

"Can't you bring the rest of the memories in?" he asked.

"I—don't know. I'm stuck on a boat somewhere in the Pacific, on my way to Australia. But the—the rest won't come in because I'm afraid it will prove that I'm Cleo."

"That's no good," he said with a touch of impatience. "You must let it come. Even if you are Cleo, it's better to know about it. We'll find out in Perth, anyway, so you might as well let yourself go."

"It isn't as easy as all that," I replied despairingly. "I'm not consciously holding back—I wouldn't."

"Yes, I know—but try and overcome it. As for the freckle that Mavis mentioned, don't take it too seriously. There's something peculiar about Mavis, anyway—something that interests me. Which reminds me that I have an appointment with her here in about five minutes, so you'd better go."

"Dear God!" I moaned. "Are you trying to make me jealous? There's nothing peculiar about Mavis. When you have a date with a fancy blonde in the middle of the night it's called a rendezvous, not a peculiarity."

"Is that another recaptured memory?" he asked, laughing at me. "Go on, run along now."

"Without Uncle Joe's lizard?"

"Never mind Uncle Joe's lizard. Aren't you going to kiss me good night?"

"What for?"

"So that I can tell the Sale boys I kissed one girl and had a rendezvous with another, all in the same night."

"Oh, nuts," I said, making for the end of the car. "Just tell them you had two rendezvous. That sounds all right."

He came along with me, holding my arm, and at the door he stopped me. "No—that wouldn't be proud enough." He bent down and, putting his arm around me, gave me a very fine kiss—the best, he explained immediately afterward, that Sale could offer.

"And very satisfactory," I conceded. "But aren't there any other boys in Sale?"

"I'll do it again sometime," he promised, with a glint in his eye, "and show you— Listen, get a move on, will you? I don't want this rendezvous to be a threesome."

"All right," I said, offended. "Have a good time. Mavis is just your type, and she'll fit perfectly into the Junior Matrons' Sewing Circle of Sale."

This struck me as being pretty funny, and I laughed all the way along the corridor of the next car. Mavis, with her bottle-washed hair, her couple of feet or so of eyelashes, and her lips painted on to suit Mavis and ignoring entirely the mouth God gave her.

When I reached my own car I found that everything was quiet. There was no sound from Uncle Joe's room, and I assumed that he must have recovered. The train flowed on, quietly and smoothly, and I remembered that the plain over which we were traveling was supposed at one time to have been completely under water. It felt, somehow, as though we were under water now.

Something moved on the floor, and I looked down just as a small lizard glided across and down the corridor. I caught my breath and stepped back, and the thing disappeared into the shadows at the end of the car.

I stood there, breathing fast and terrified that the creature would come back—and then I noticed that it had left tracks where it had crossed the corridor. I stooped over and looked curiously, and saw that the tracks were made with blood.

Chapter Fourteen
MURDER!

I STRAIGHTENED UP SLOWLY, frowning at the red smears and feeling a little frightened. The creature must be wounded, I thought vaguely— and yet it had seemed perfectly all right.

As I stood there it glided out of the shadows at the end of the corridor and came toward me. I backed away in a panic, and as soon as I moved, it stopped. It remained absolutely still for a moment, and then the small body bulged, the tiny mouth opened, and the thing barked like a dog.

It was too much for me. I turned and fled, and I had reached the end of the corridor in the next car before I came to a stop and pulled myself together.

Serves me right, I thought crossly. *I ought to be in bed, anyway*—it was almost three o'clock. I should have gone to bed when Aunt Esther went out to attend to Uncle Joe. But I shuddered, and was suddenly thankful that I hadn't, because that lizard must have been in the compartment then—right in there with me. I heard it barking. And how could a lizard bark like a dog, anyway?

But this was Australia, and there were all kinds of queer animals and birds. The kangaroo and the emu, and those little teddy bears— the koalas—and, queerest of all, the four-legged fur-bearing creature with webbed feet, a bill like a duck, and that laid eggs and then suckled its young. Platypus—the duck-billed platypus. So why not a lizard that barked?

I pushed my hair off my forehead, rerolled my sweater sleeves, and started back. I was going to bed, and I intended to forget all about the lizard. It was an Australian lizard, and barking was undoubtedly one of its accomplishments, but that was no reason why I should be afraid of it.

I walked back to my car, where I hesitated at Wilfred's door. I ought to tell him about the creature—they had been searching for it, and anyway, I knew I'd sleep better if somehow I had it safely shut away.

I knocked timidly, and Wilfred opened the door immediately. "What is it?" he whispered, fumbling to pull his shabby bathrobe more tightly around him.

"The lizard," I whispered back. "It's out here in the hall."

"Oh—goodo." He came out and closed the door quietly behind him.

"How's Uncle Joe?"

"He's sleeping now," Wilfred said, blinking in trip light, "but these attacks are pretty bad, and he might wake up again—although we hope he's over it now. Mother and I are going to insist on his going to a doctor when we get back to Perth. After all, how does he know it's only indigestion? It might be heart, or something of that sort."

He had been moving slowly along the corridor with his head bent, and he suddenly stooped over and said, "Got him." He put the thing into his pocket and came back. "Uncle Joe will be glad."

"It—it barks," I said, feeling foolish.

"Oh yes—one of those barking lizards from the Nullarbor Plain. Uncle picked it up on the way over."

"We're on the plain now," I said, glancing out the window.

Wilfred pulled his watch from the pocket of his bathrobe and consulted it gravely. "Yes—we must be. But why aren't you in bed?"

"I'm just going—only I want you to look at this. That lizard tracked some blood over the corridor here."

Wilfred stooped over and examined the drying smears. "That's funny," he said in a puzzled voice. "It does look like blood." He looked up and down the corridor, as though an explanation might be hanging on one of the doors, and then shrugged. "I don't see how it can be blood. The lizard doesn't seem to be injured, and if anyone had been hurt, we'd surely have heard about it. It might be paint—red paint."

"Oh—of course." I hadn't thought of paint, and I felt relieved. "I'll bet that's what it is."

"We're all right in here," Wilfred said, indicating his own compartment. "I'll just have a look at Mary and Eileen."

He knocked rather timidly on the door, and the Belle of Beaconsfield answered him with a certain amount of irritation.

"Of course we're all right. What do you want to come waking us up in the middle of the night for? Go back to bed, for heaven's sake, and stop being an old woman."

"All right, dear—I was just checking up." He came back to me and stated superfluously, "They're all right."

I nodded and said good night to him, and he disappeared quietly into his own compartment. I was a bit annoyed with him for having satisfied himself about his own immediate family and leaving it at that, and I had a vague, uneasy feeling that I should check up on everyone else in the car. But it would mean knocking on all the doors, and probably half of them would swear at me—and anyway, those tracks were probably red paint. I gave it up and went into my own compartment.

Aunt Esther was in bed again, her body lying neatly under the bedclothes and her head in the shadow from the upper berth. I thought of turning on the light, to make sure that she was all right, and then decided against it. The light would wake her, and she had already been disturbed once.

The shade was still up, and I looked out over the plain. It was a silvered fairyland of gnomes and pixies, I thought idly—and then remembered Uncle Joe's lizard. There were no fairies in the bush—only barking lizards and other curious Australian creatures. Like the bird that laughed—the laughing jackass. Only he wasn't out there on the plain—not that I knew of, anyway. He was in the Blue Mountains—places where there were trees. Not like this treeless plain. How smoothly the train moved, like floating through a mass of silver seaweed.

I shivered from head to foot, shook my head vigorously, and climbed into the upper berth.

What was the use of getting undressed? I thought wearily. I didn't care how I crumpled my clothes—they were rotten clothes, anyhow—and I didn't want to wake Aunt Esther. She might as well sleep, I reflected, sighing—I knew I couldn't. I'd slept myself out during the afternoon, and anyway, all those memories were waiting just outside the door.

I relaxed my body and made an effort to remember things—but somehow they wouldn't come that way. Instead I started to wonder how I knew the names of so many of the Australian animals and birds. Birds. The beautiful white peacock.

I moved my head restlessly and fretted a little because I hadn't turned the light on and had a look at Aunt Esther. But surely nothing could have happened to her, lying peacefully in bed.

Perhaps Bill had told me about the animals and birds—but Bill was a blank wall, and I gave him up. I thought of flowers, and knew that I was supposed to look for Sturt's desert pea—red and purplish black. And then, in Western Australia, I must study the everlastings, and the geraniums which grew so profusely on bushes. They were almost a weed—the geraniums.

I rubbed my hand slowly across my forehead, and then I remembered. Old John was standing there and telling me what to do on the trip—what to look for. I could hear his voice, but I couldn't exactly see him. Who was he, anyway? John—Old John. He was my employer—interested in my trip and telling me what to see and what I should study.

My head began to ache, and I felt that I didn't want to think any more. I turned over and wondered why Aunt Esther, lying beneath me, was so still. How could she sleep so well on a moving train—and with Uncle Joe's illness on her mind? I thought of the lizard. It must have been in our compartment all the afternoon, since I had twice heard it bark in here—and then, when it did come out, it was tracking blood.

I felt cold into the bone, and I began to tremble slightly. I should have looked at her before; I'd have to look now—I'd have to make sure she was all right. I raised myself on a wobbly elbow, but I could not find a light switch, and at last I hung my head over the side and peered down below me. The bottom of the lower berth was sharply clear in the moonlight, and the shadowed head was more visible than when I had stood on the floor, although I could not see her properly. But she did not look right to me—there was something—And then it came to me—her hair. Aunt Esther had black hair, and this seemed to be white.

My teeth were chattering by this time, and for a moment I could not muster up strength to climb down to the floor. From the corner of my eye I could see the ghostly bushes gliding past the window, and I had a queer, scared feeling of being alone with them and with a woman whose hair had turned white.

I swallowed a scream and fumbled out of the berth and down to the door. I avoided looking out of the window or at Aunt Esther while I groped for the light, but when I had it on I swung around and forced my eyes into the lower berth.

It wasn't Aunt Esther lying there—it was Mavis. She stared at me impersonally from half-opened eyes that looked like bits of blue glass—and her throat had been cut from ear to ear.

Chapter Fifteen
NOT A WOUND—

I FOUND MYSELF out in the corridor, screaming. A conductor came first, and he looked at me and then peered into the compartment. He began to scold me about the shade being up, and then he went in and became, suddenly, very quiet.

Aunt Esther and Wilfred came out of Uncle Joe's compartment, and Wilfred was asking rather wildly, "What is it? Good God, what is it?"

I could not talk, but I pointed, and they walked in after the conductor. Mary poked her head out of her door, her hair in curlers and her eyes wide and scared. Jimmy and his roommate emerged, decently encased in dressing-robes. And then people seemed to come from all directions. I was conscious of Jimmy, close beside me, muttering, "What has happened? What is it?" but he seemed to fade away after a while, and the whole confused picture slid off into darkness.

When I opened my eyes again I was lying comfortably in a lower berth. There was no one with me, but the light was on, and the water carafe rattled cheerfully in its niche. I watched it idly for a while, and then the train slowed up and stopped, and I wondered where we were. Perhaps not at any station, I thought, remembering with a quick, gasping little breath. They were doing something about that poor girl Mavis. Her throat—

I shuddered from head to foot and then started violently as someone opened the door. It was Aunt Esther, and she came in, followed by the conductor.

"How do you feel?" she asked, while her fingers felt for my wrist and lingered there.

I supposed my pulse was jumping like a scared rabbit, but I answered quietly enough, "I'm all right. Please tell me what happened in there."

"We don't really know—but the guard, here, would like to hear your story, if you feel well enough to tell it."

"I feel quite well enough, but there isn't much to tell. I thought you were lying in that berth, Aunt Esther, and I didn't turn on the light, because I didn't want to disturb you. I—I was lying right above her—I didn't know—"

"You undressed in the dark?" the conductor put in flatly.

"No—no, I didn't undress at all. I was restless, and I just lay down on the berth. I couldn't see her properly—I didn't know—"

Aunt Esther touched my wrist again and then looked up at the conductor. "You'll have to go—she's had a shock. I'll stay with her now, and the trooper can speak to her later, if he wants, when she's feeling better."

He backed out under her crisp decisiveness, and she closed the door firmly behind him and then came back to sit beside me.

"What compartment is this?" I asked feebly.

"It's Jimmy's. He and the other man will move to another—the guard is arranging it. I don't wonder you fainted, Cleo—that's terrible in there—dreadful."

"But where were you?" I asked, turning my head restlessly. "I thought it was you there all the time."

"I was sitting in with Joe. He'd had a very nasty turn, and I thought he'd be bad all night. He thinks it's indigestion, you know, but I'm convinced it's his heart. I don't know what's the matter with him lately, anyway—he used to go to the doctor regularly, and now, when I think there's something really wrong, he won't budge."

I murmured some response, but I couldn't really get my mind away from Mavis. After a moment I whispered, "She's—dead?"

Aunt Esther said, "Mercy, child! Of course. You saw her."

Tears began to slide out of the corners of my eyes, and I mopped at them absently with the top of the sheet, because I couldn't find a handkerchief. "She couldn't have done it herself," I said presently. "Not Mavis—she was so full of life."

"Oh, no indeed," Aunt Esther replied quietly. "It was done for her. Murder."

"I wonder how she came to be in our room. What was she doing there?"

"Lord knows," said Aunt Esther, and shrugged.

I was quiet for a minute or two, and then I began to think about Clive. Where was he? He had had an appointment with Mavis.

"Did Clive show up?" I asked, and caught a look of embarrassment on Aunt Esther's face. "He had a date to meet Mavis in the lounge car," I added, and saw her face clear.

"Oh yes—I didn't know whether you knew. He told us that. He came along after you fainted in the corridor out there, and he carried you in here—but the guard wouldn't let him stay. They wanted him in there, you know. He said he and Mavis had a private matter to discuss, but he wouldn't say what. So you knew about it?"

"Yes. Do you know whether they had their talk?"

"He says not. Said he got tired of waiting, and so came along and ran into us."

The train began to move, and I sat up, holding my spinning head in my hands. "We didn't stop long. You'd think, somehow, that all this would delay us for days."

Aunt Esther shook her head. "These stations are just small settlements, made up chiefly of train crews. There wouldn't be any stations on the plain if they were not needed for the trains. There is sometimes a trooper at these stations—Australian mounted police, you know—and I expect we'll have picked one up."

I thought of the bush and glanced quickly at the window, but the shade was drawn.

"How far through the plain are we?" I asked.

"Oh—we won't be through until tomorrow afternoon sometime."

I got off the bed, and she asked quickly, "Where are you going?"

"I don't know—but I can't just lie there."

There was an abrupt rap on the door, and it opened to reveal Jimmy and a tall, sunburned man in uniform.

"Cleo," Jimmy said, "this is Sergeant Cronlin of the troopers. He wants to talk to you and Aunt Esther."

The huge Cronlin came into the small room and seemed to fill it.

"Easy on, miss—I just want to ask a few questions about that girl in there."

I felt a bit like a rat in a trap, but Cronlin was courteous, and, unexpectedly, I found it easy to talk to him. He led me through the events of the night, which was simple enough, but when he asked if I had ever seen Mavis before this trip I was up against my cloudy memory and I could not be sure. As a matter of fact, I had a nagging idea that I *had* seen her before, but in the end I said to Cronlin, "Not that I know of," and he seemed satisfied. I did not mention my loss of memory, and I had to give my name as Cleo Ballister, which bothered me.

Aunt Esther was questioned, and answered briefly that she had never seen Mavis before m her life, and that she had spent the evening with her brother-in-law, who had been ill.

The trooper said, "Well, thanks very much. You'd better stay in here—this gentleman will move his things, and then I'll let you bring what you need from that other compartment."

Jimmy began to get his things together, while the trooper watched. When he had finished the roommate came in and began to bang his belongings into a battered suitcase. He was annoyed at being thrown out of his compartment, and said so, using the adjective "bloody" after every three or four words, until the trooper stirred and boomed out, "All right, all right—less of it"— which shut him up completely.

After he had gone Cronlin escorted us to our former compartment to get our things. Mavis was still there, covered with a sheet, and I stumbled around, trying to keep my eyes away from her.

Aunt Esther, composedly and efficiently packing her suitcase, nodded at the sheeted figure and asked, "You're not going to leave her here?"

Cronlin said they would carry her forward to luggage as soon as law and order had been restored in the train.

Aunt Esther murmured something about the heat, but Cronlin's tanned face remained impassive, and presently we finished our packing and left. He followed us and then, with his hand on the door latch, said, "Sure you have your own purses? We can't find hers."

We both checked with a hasty glance and then nodded, and Cronlin locked the door and escorted us to our new quarters. Just before he left us there he ran me over with a cool, impersonal eye and observed, "I still can't make out why you didn't get undressed tonight."

"I don't know myself," I said impatiently. "I guess I just hadn't bothered. I was restless, and anyway, I hate undressing on trains—you're so cramped for space."

He did not press it any further, but went off and left us to our own devices.

We were busy for a while, settling our things, and then I asked, "Did Wilfred give the lizard to Uncle Joe?"

Aunt Esther nodded. "Joe was delighted—he said to thank you no end. He'd have hated losing it."

"How did he take it—about Mavis?"

"Oh well—not too badly. He was shocked, of course, and he couldn't seem to stop talking about it, but I gave him one of his sleeping pills and he dropped off almost at once."

"I'm glad of that. Is Eileen all right?"

Aunt Esther smiled. "Mary wouldn't let her out of the compartment and refused to let anyone talk to her. She wouldn't come out herself, any farther than to stick her nose through the door. She was terrified. Kept saying there must be a lunatic running around in the train."

I said, "Oh God! Is our door locked?"

It wasn't, because at that moment it opened and Clive walked in. He said, "Oh, here you are—I've been looking for you. Cleo, will you come outside for a moment? I want to talk to you."

Aunt Esther moved between us and said firmly, "No. She's safer in here, and in any case, she needs a rest."

Clive looked at me and then stepped over and took my wrist. I supposed my pulse was still jumping as before—I felt like that, anyway. He looked over my head at Aunt Esther and then nodded and dropped my wrist.

He did not go immediately, however, but stopped at the door, with his hand on the latch.

"That poor girl Mavis, you know—"

"The trouble with her," Aunt Esther interrupted frostily, "was that she was too forward. That kind always get into trouble. I think you had better go—my niece must have some rest."

"Yes, of course. It was just that there was an odd thing about the girl." His eyes strayed to mine and held then. "She must have been in some previous accident, because her arm was strapped up. Not a wound, you know—strain of some sort."

Chapter Sixteen
AMERICAN PASSPORT

IT TOOK ME A MINUTE OR TWO, after Clive had gone, to realize the full implication of what he had said. Mavis was Virginia Peters, the girl who had traveled with me from Sydney and who had hurt her arm. She must have followed up quickly, then, taken another name, and said nothing to me about who she was. I frowned and shook my head. I didn't believe it—it must be a coincidence.

"Men are exasperating at times," Aunt Esther said, pouring water from the carafe into a glass. "What on earth do we care about her arm being strapped up? Here, you take off your clothes and get to bed. I'm going to give you one of Joe's sleeping pills."

I obeyed, feeling hazily thankful at having someone to tell me what to do, so that I need not think for myself. After I had taken the pill I settled back into the pillow and watched Aunt Esther puttering around, but when she switched off the light and raised the shade I turned over and faced the wall, so that I could not see the bush.

Suppose it wasn't coincidence, and Mavis really was that other girl? Then I wasn't Cleo—she was—and she had kept quiet about it because Cleo Ballister was in a spot. She had tried to convince me that I was Cleo by mentioning that freckle, too.

I took a long breath that went out again in little quivers. My name wasn't Cleo, anyway—it was Gin. But how could that be right? How could anyone be called Gin? Old John—Old John dabbled in flowers and animals, and he was in Sydney—and he always called me Gin. Then I must be Virginia Peters, because Gin was short for Ginny. They'd have to stop calling me Gin, though—I didn't like it. And they'd have to stop calling me Cleo, because I wouldn't stand for it.

I began to have an uneasy feeling that the ghost bushes were staring at my back, and at last I could not stand it any longer and had to turn over. I looked at the window and was filled with an instant sense of relief and peace. The plain was no longer washed in spectral, tantalizing silver, but lay flat and gray and quiet under the dawn. Far away, on the horizon, there was a faint pink glow. I should watch the sunrise, I thought contentedly, it ought to be wonderful—and went off into profound sleep.

I came up through what seemed layers of heavy blackness, much later, to find Aunt Esther prodding at me determinedly.

"Goodness," she said, "those pills of Joe's work well on you—I was beginning to be uneasy. I've been trying to get you awake for nearly ten minutes. You've missed morning tea, and I doubt whether you can get your shower bath now—and if you don't hurry, you'll miss breakfast too."

I did get my shower bath. As soon as Aunt Esther mentioned it I knew I'd have to have it—it was more important to me than breakfast. The attendant was a bit annoyed about it, but I pleaded and bullied until he gave in. I hurried into my clothes and then raced in to breakfast, to find that they had saved a seat for me. Uncle Joe had been late too, it appeared, and Aunt Esther and Wilfred were seated with him. Mary and Eileen had finished, and Clive and Jimmy were not in sight, but the dining-car was still fairly well filled, and I noticed Cronlin sitting at one of the tables.

Uncle Joe was giving out free theories.

"Now take a girl like that—she puts her coils around the men and leads them up the garden path—just playing with them and human nature being what it is, one of them finally explodes and takes his revenge."

Aunt Esther asked, "Who?"

"Well, that I don't know," Uncle Joe admitted. "But she was so used to that sort of thing that she even played up to me." He paused for a modest laugh. "Tried to get me to make an appointment with her in Perth. Suggested one of these night clubs. I told her an old cove like I am wouldn't know anything about night clubs, but she said she'd find out for me and promised to give me a good time."

Wilfred, silent and progressively uncomfortable through this, now spoke up bravely: "I don't think we should dwell on the bad points of one who has passed away."

Since these were Uncle Joe's sentiments, more or less, he looked a bit dashed for a moment—but he soon recovered. He fixed an eye on Wilfred and said belligerently, "I'm not blaming the girl. She liked to have a jolly time, and she always wanted someone to have it with her, that's all."

"Someone who would pay the bill," Wilfred supplied thinly.

Aunt Esther frowned at him and said, "That's no way to talk."

"No, by Jove, it isn't." Uncle Joe backed her up, getting his revenge. "The dead should be allowed to rest in peace."

Wilfred changed the subject. "We shall have to put our watches back again soon—between Rawlinna and Kitchener, I believe."

"Who cares?" I said absently, and as their eyes turned to me, with brows raised all around, I added hastily, "I mean—this dreadful thing— it's hard to remember everyday matters like—like watches."

Aunt Esther came to my rescue. "That Cronlin wants to talk to you directly after breakfast."

"But he's already talked to us," I protested, feeling my stomach turn over.

"Well, he wants to go through it again. He's trying to find out why she was murdered in our compartment."

"That much I want to know myself," I muttered.

"He says it looks mighty fishy to him," Aunt Esther added calmly.

"What's 'e talking about?" Uncle Joe thundered. "Of course it looks fishy."

I looked at them and wondered what they would think if they knew what I hoped and believed was the truth—that Mavis was Cleo Ballister, their niece and cousin.

Could Jimmy have killed her? I wondered, swallowing too-hot coffee. But why? He didn't know she was Cleo, and even if he had known, why kill the goose he expected to lay a golden egg for him?

I closed my mind up and devoted myself to my breakfast. Clive came in after a while and tried to sit at our table by putting a chair in the aisle but one of the waiters fought it out with him and finally placed him with a clergyman at the next table—where he immediately got into a religious argument.

Uncle Joe chewed at his mustache in a worried fashion and said, "What's the matter with him this morning? He's full of the Old Nick."

"They say doctors are inclined to let loose when they're on holiday," Wilfred explained. "It's the confined sort of life they lead."

"Ah, teach your grannie," Uncle Joe said rudely. "You never let loose in your life—so how would you know?"

Wilfred took offense at this remark, and Aunt Esther along with him. They showed it by folding their mouths into thin lines and opening them only to put food in.

Uncle Joe left them to it and turned to me. "Well, young'un, how do you like your Austrylian cousins?"

I glanced automatically at Aunt Esther and saw her mouth quiver as she resisted the impulse to say "Australian."

"Very much," I said to Uncle Joe courteously.

"Goodo. Just for that I'll buy you a fur coat. Musquash."

"Come again?" I said, still courteous.

"Eh?"

"I thought you said musquash."

"That's it," said Uncle Joe nearby. "Musquash it is."

"Well, thanks—thanks a lot," I murmured doubtfully.

The voices of Clive and the clergyman intruded on us at this point—raised, somewhat strained, but still gentlemanly. Uncle Joe tried to get into the argument but was drowned out, so he finished his third cup of tea—noisily—and poured another one.

I looked out at the scenery. The bush was still there, but by daylight they were just bushes, some with a bluish tinge to the leaves. It was desert land that stretched tiresomely, as far as the eye could see.

"Let's go," I suggested restlessly.

"Right you are," Uncle Joe agreed. "Only where'll we go to, eh?" He laughed heartily and chucked me under the chin.

"Cronlin told us to go to your compartment, Joe," Aunt Esther said.

"Ahh, let him find us—what do they pay him for? C'mon, we'll go to the lounge car."

He heaved himself up and started to make for the door with his table napkin still dangling from one of the buttonholes of his waistcoat. He didn't notice it, but plowed on, with the rest of us following in his wake. He didn't get away with the napkin, however, as a waiter detached it neatly while he was passing. Uncle Joe looked down, said, " 'Ere, 'ere!" and then, "Oh," in understanding.

As we approached our car he remembered to thank me for finding his lizard, and then decided to get the creature and do some work on his new painting.

I heard Aunt Esther draw an exasperated little sigh. "You finished that new one last night, Joe— I saw it."

Uncle Joe, in a fine fury, flung into his compartment and shuffled through a suitcase until he found the picture. It was finished, all right, and he stared at it for some time and then looked up at us. His face was a dark red and his forehead veined.

"Who did this?" he asked thickly.

Nobody answered, and I felt uncomfortable and sorry for him.

He looked down at the picture again and said slowly, "I wouldn't make a muck of the thing like this, Esther—you know I wouldn't. Somebody's been playing tricks on me."

"Why would anyone do such a silly thing?" Aunt Esther asked patiently.

Uncle Joe flung the block back into the suitcase and pushed past us.

"All right, have it your own way. I suppose you think I'm a loony, but I know someone's playing a trick on me, and when I catch him he'll be bloody sorry."

He went off in the direction of the lounge car, and Aunt Esther and Wilfred followed, looking disturbed. I let them go and then slipped into my compartment.

In less than ten minutes Clive had joined me and was looking unusually serious.

"I'm glad to find you alone. This affair is beginning to look pretty bad."

"Was Mavis Cleo Ballister?" I asked directly.

"I don't know. The arm tallies with the information I got from that hospital—but I wish we could find her purse."

"We?"

"Cronlin and I. I'm the only doctor on the train, so I've been giving him a hand. I suppose he'll turn it over to the police at Kalgoorlie."

"Oh dear," I said, "I hope we won't be delayed. I haven't much time, and I'm supposed to study the Western Australia geraniums."

Clive looked up quickly and asked, "What's that?"

"I—I don't know," I told him confusedly. "I'm secretary to a man I call 'Old John,' and he's a naturalist. He calls me Gin, and I guess it must be short for Virginia."

"Can't you get the rest of it?" he asked anxiously. "You should, if you can remember that much."

"No—yes, I think it's coming. I know I'm not Cleo Ballister."

But he shook his head a little. "Don't be too sure. You might be so anxious not to be Cleo that your mind is remembering things that never happened."

"Oh, please—"

"If we could only find that purse," he said grimly. "There might be a passport in it."

"Let's look for it," I suggested eagerly. "It must be somewhere."

Clive glanced about with a rather defeated expression. "Cronlin has been around with a fine-tooth comb. Her compartment and her luggage, your aunt's luggage and yours, and your former compartment he even went through Miss Hogg's stuff."

"Miss *Hogg?*"

"Mavis's roommate. She was in a wax, too. Threatened to sue the Trans-Australian for putting her in with a loose woman."

"How did she know Mavis was loose?" I asked.

"Said she could tell by the color of her hair."

"Some guesser," I said, and opened my purse to get a cigarette. The interior of the vast red bag seemed to be unduly cluttered, and after a moment's fumbling I pulled out a small navy-blue envelope pocketbook.

After one breathless moment of gaping I tore it open. There was an American passport, and I clawed at the cover and exposed the photograph inside.

Mavis. Mavis, with a pretty smile and all her blond curls neatly in place.

Chapter Seventeen
UNLUCKY PENNY

I WAS BITTERLY DISAPPOINTED. I must be Cleo, then—and after the accident Virginia Peters, for some reason, had changed her name, left the hospital, and hurried to Melbourne so that she could catch the train on which I was traveling. She had changed the color of her hair and had said nothing to me about our knowing each other. But why? I knew that Mrs. Bunton had mentioned her hair as being brown and had said it was either slightly darker or slightly lighter than mine—I couldn't remember which. I was pretty sure that Mavis would not have had time to go to a hairdresser in Melbourne, and that meant that she had blended her curls on the train. It would be difficult, I thought, but not impossible.

Clive took the passport from my hand and studied it for some time in silence, and then he closed it up and handed it back to me.

"We'll have to give the purse to Cronlin. Where shall we say we found it?"

"I don't know," I said tiredly. "What does it matter, anyway? If I'm Cleo, I deserve all that's coming to me."

He ignored that and muttered, "We'll have to be quick. Let's see—the lounge—that's it. I'll take it along to the lounge and find it there."

He went out, and I fell to thinking about Old John and Gin. Somehow I didn't think that Gin was just wishful thinking—if it were, surely I'd have made it Ginny. But perhaps all those memories that had come back to me were false—perhaps they were all pictures that my brain had made up.

No, I thought, *those things are real—I never made them up—and even if I am Cleo Ballister, I never pushed that poor old man down the stairs.*

But there was that passport picture of Mavis—you couldn't get around that. Unless, of course, she pasted it in herself and tore the other one out!

I began to feel better at once. She could have substituted that picture of herself—one that showed her with blond hair and that had been taken before she made the brown-haired trip from Sydney.

I relaxed back against the seat and looked out of the window. Still no trees—just scrubby bushes, desert land, with hard, brilliant, hot sunlight. And then I saw three camels. Their backs were loaded, and they were connected by ropes stretching from one tail to the next nose. Two of them had a man perched precariously in among the load. *It's a camel train,* I thought, *and Old John told me I would probably see one.* Old John with his white goatee and hatfuls of money—and he spent his time doing fool things like studying geraniums.

There was a smart rap at the door, and I opened it to feel immediately dwarfed by Cronlin's huge frame.

"Nice day, miss," he said courteously.

I allowed that it was, and he added, "I've been in the lounge car talking to various people."

I said I hoped he'd had a good time, and his eyes narrowed slightly in his tanned face.

"I'm told you broke your engagement because of this girl Virginia Peters?"

I swallowed air under his steady gaze, and he said, "Surprised?"

"Well—I thought—"

He shook his head. "Her name was Virginia Peters, all right. Found her purse in the lounge car, and any number of people identified it—said they'd seen her carrying it around—and her passport was in it. What I want to find out now is why she called herself Mavis Montague."

"Why would anybody?" I asked, and had a helpless feeling that I was making a very bad impression. I added hastily, "Do you know anything about her? About Virginia Peters, I mean?"

"I'll telegraph for information from Rawlinna," he said, keeping his eyes on my face. "We'll be pulling in shortly. I want to have that all cut and dried by the time we reach Kalgoorlie. Just now I'd like you to tell me about that scene in the diner yesterday."

"What scene?" I asked in a scared voice.

"When that girl and the doctor walked in, and you broke your engagement with him."

"But that—I was only joking," I said uneasily, and wondered whether I was supposed to have killed Mavis because I was jealous.

"Later on you said that she was an old friend of yours."

"Oh no—I mean, it was only that she was an American, like myself."

Cronlin said, "I see," without much inflection, and added, "Are you still engaged to the doctor, then?

I thought I had better be and said quickly, "Yes—yes, of course."

"Did you know that he had an appointment with the girl in the lounge car late last night?"

"Yes, I knew about that." I was beginning to feel like a tightrope walker and decided that brevity was my safest course.

"Do you know the reason for the appointment?

"No."

"Don't you think it odd for a man to make such an appointment when he was engaged to someone else?"

I laughed, and hoped it didn't sound too much like hysteria. "Oh, listen! I'll bet you had dates with other girls when you were engaged."

If he was amused, he concealed it well. "The purse," he said, remaining deadpan, "was found in the lounge car, where your fiance was waiting for her—and he says she never turned up."

I went deadpan myself. "My fiance," I said gloomily, "never tells a lie."

He sighed, shifted his great body, and held on to his patience. "How was it that she was murdered in your compartment?"

"I don't know—I'd have told you if I did."

"Why were you not in the compartment yourself? Where were you?"

"I was here and there," I said, and proceeded to tell him about the barking lizard. "If I'd known there was such a thing, it would have been different—but I was scared stiff, and I didn't want to stay in the compartment alone. If my aunt hadn't been called to attend to my uncle, I'd have gone to bed and to sleep."

"Your uncle—Mr. Joseph Ballister—he's not quite right, is he?"

"Who told you that?" I asked sharply.

"It's true, isn't it?"

"Certainly not," I said angrily. "He's perfectly normal."

"You must know that he keeps painting pictures and then forgetting all about it in a few hours."

"Someone is playing a mean joke on him."

"How do you know?" Cronlin snapped.

I shrugged. I didn't know, of course.

He turned to go and said, "Well, thanks very much, miss. I see we're getting into Rawlinna, and I'll be busy for a while."

He strode away, and I looked out of the window and decided to get off the train and stretch my legs. It was midday, and the sun was very hot, but it was a relief to walk around on solid ground.

Clive appeared after a while and came and put a newspaper over my head. "You don't want that dome of yours to get any crazier than it is already."

"I don't know," I said. "I'm just sane enough to be miserable now—maybe if I could get a little crazier, I'd be happy."

"Oh well," said Clive, being philosophical about it, because it wasn't his brains that were addled. "We'll have some information soon. Cronlin's in there now, burning up the wires."

"Yes, I know—all about Virginia Peters. I wish we could find out about it when he gets it—even if we have to tell him all."

"We may have to tell him all, at that," Clive said thoughtfully. "Do you know whom he suspects?"

"Yes," I sighed. "You and me—and Uncle Joe."

Clive nodded. "But if you want the truth, it's mostly you. Cronlin inclines to the jealousy motive."

"Well, I don't know that I blame him," I said, and found that I was close to tears. "If I were Cleo, I would suspect myself too."

"You still think that you're not Cleo?" he asked curiously.

I frowned and jerked my head away, and the newspaper fell off. He stooped to pick it up, and I watched him, thinking that evidently he still believed I was Cleo—the passport must have convinced him.

We went back to the train, and Clive said, "Come on down to the lounge car. We might still get elevenses."

"Get what?"

"Tea."

"God almighty!" I moaned. "It's a wonder you people don't drown in that dishwater. Early morning tea, tea at breakfast, tea at eleven, tea with lunch, afternoon tea, tea with dinner, tea before going to bed."

"Sometimes we don't get them all in," he admitted mildly.

Uncle Joe was waltzing Matilda again in the lounge car, and Eileen was singing it for him in a shrill treble. She had pitched it a bit too high and was having trouble, but she solved the problem by suddenly plunging down two whole octaves. This put Uncle Joe off, and he stopped and asked her what she thought she was doing. Instead of answering him, she said good morning to us, and Clive asked, "Any tea around?"

Aunt Esther came out of a magazine and said, "There was, but they've cleared it away."

"I don't know what you're going to do," I said to Clive. "And lunch an hour away."

Cronlin brushed past us and approached a woman who sat reading in one of the chairs. She was sallow and wore spectacles, and her hair was done in what appeared to be a series of birds' nests.

"Miss Hogg," said Cronlin, sitting down beside her, "could you tell me—"

"I'll tell you nothing," she interrupted, glaring through the spectacles. "I ignored the girl as completely as possible, and I resent any suggestion that her affairs were in any way known to me. The company shall hear of this, you may be sure. Allowing a person of that type to travel first class!"

Cronlin, possibly tainted by my flippancies, said that undoubtedly the company should have made Miss Peters run along behind the train. "But since they didn't, I'm afraid you'll have to answer a few questions. For instance, do you know whether this belonged to her?"

He opened his palm and displayed Cleo Ballister's lucky penny.

Chapter Eighteen
ON THE SPOT

MISS HOGG BARELY GLANCED at the shoddy little brooch, but Eileen squealed, "There it is! Look, Auntie Cleo, there's the penny!"

Cronlin turned his head, and I stepped forward, feeling confused and embarrassed.

"Why, so it is," I said, stooping over to examine the thing. "My lucky penny." I showed Cronlin my purse and the tear where the brooch had been ripped away. "I can't imagine why she'd want to steal it from me, though."

"No—nor can I," said Cronlin grimly, and stood up. He left the car, and Clive, after a moment's hesitation, turned and followed him. I stood where I was with a feeling that my doom was sealed.

Uncle Joe came and patted me on the back. "All right, old girl—keep your chin up. These things have to happen sometimes, but don't you take it too seriously. If she took your penny, she must have wanted it for something—and Cronlin can suspect that she ripped it off while you were murdering her, if he likes. We know it isn't true."

"Joe, *please!*" Aunt Esther cried. "You ought to keep your mouth closed, upon my word you should!"

Uncle Joe turned on her. "I'm only figuring what Cronlin will think, Es, that's all. But we needn't worry much, anyway—chap's only a trooper, and he'll hand in his report at Kalgoorlie."

"I don't want him to hand me in at Kalgoorlie," I said weakly.

"Don't you worry, my girl—nothing to worry about. Of course I hope they won't hold any of us up there—rotten place to spend Christmas. I like Christmas at me own home."

"You bought me a lot of presents, didn't you, Uncle Joe?" Eileen asked happily.

Aunt Esther said, "Eileen!" and Miss Hogg rose to the surface with an opinion. "That child is old enough to be taught manners."

"I beg your pardon, madam," said Uncle Joe furiously, "but our Eileen is very much the lady."

Miss Hogg retired to her magazine before the menace m his voice, and a large woman, two seats down, boomed out, "You are quite right, Mr. Ballister. She is a little lady."

Eileen preened herself but had finesse enough to say nothing. Miss Hogg's magazine quivered.

Uncle Joe blew his nose, put his handkerchief away, and said thoughtfully, "The worst of it is that this murder took place in South Australia, and Cronlin is a South Australia trooper. Now it seems to me that anyone called as a witness might be taken off the train at the next stop—Kitchener, that would be—get there about 'arf-parss twelve—and that's where we meet the Trans-Australian going in the other direction—and perhaps we'll be bundled onto her and taken back into South Australia. See?"

We saw—with various unhappy reactions. Miss Hogg took it harder than anyone, and she finally left the car, declaring that she would write the Queen—who she said was more or less of a personal friend of hers, as they had met at a large reception in Melbourne, when the Queen was visiting as Duchess of York.

Since I didn't know why I was crossing the continent anyway, I wasn't particularly upset about being headed back again—except for the fact that it, would mean another night on the plain, among the ghostly bushes. I thought of the lucky penny and felt a surge of hope. If Mavis had stolen it from me, she must be Cleo Ballister—who was convinced that she would have no luck without it. But apparently she had not wanted to be known as Cleo, and so she had used my passport. I felt sure now that it was mine and that Cronlin would soon have information that proved it. Mavis must have torn out the picture of me and pasted in one of herself.

I took a long breath of relief and tried to concentrate on Old John and Aunt Shep. What was Aunt Shep's last name, for instance? Shep—Sheppherd, of course. Only I had always called her Aunt Shep, and I had no idea of her first name. There must be a great many Sheppherds in Los Angeles.

Jimmy wandered in and dropped down beside me. He was pale and he looked worried, and when he put a match to his cigarette his hand shook.

I noticed that Aunt Esther was talking with the woman who had the booming voice, while Uncle Joe was picking out a tune on the piano with one finger. Eileen, to prove her ladylike qualities, sat quietly studying a fashion magazine, with her two little fingers curved out elegantly.

Jimmy leaned toward me and murmured, "God! You've a nerve of iron! I don't know why you did it, though."

"Did what? What are you talking about now?" I gasped.

He laughed, although his eyes were serious. "You'd never admit anything, would you? Not even to me." His cigarette crumpled suddenly in his fingers, and he muttered, "I'm mad about you."

Clive came back and lounged into a seat close to us. I felt as though my face must be a pale green, and I hastily brought out powder and lipstick and went to work on it. When I had finished I caught Clive's eye and thought it held a certain amount of disapproval.

"Oh well," I sighed at him, "don't worry too much. I wouldn't do this in Sale—or anyway, not at the church social."

Jimmy laughed, and Clive squinted his eyes at me. "I hope I can depend on that. I expect to be an elder when I get back, and there are certain strict 'don'ts' for elders' wives."

"They all have to have shiny noses," I agreed. "That's one of the 'musts.' "

But I had stepped on the toes of the lady with the booming voice. She boomed afresh. "I beg your pardon, young lady, but is my nose shining?"

"No," I said, "it isn't. But if you are a church elder's wife, I expect it is a large, fashionable church. We are speaking of the little white church in a village not long risen from the primeval mud."

She nodded, satisfied. "But don't let them frighten you into a shiny nose, a bun of hair at the back of your neck, and a tweed coat and skirt that look as though they had been worn by a camel, my dear. These small towns are far too insular. Just you stick to your own ideas, and you'll do those people a world of good."

"Look," said Clive patiently. "Neither of you knows Sale—that's very evident. Sale is far from being insular—and of course the girls use makeup. As for their clothes—matter of fact, they look a good deal smarter than the city girls. They mostly make their own clothes, and they're onto all the latest angles—"

Jimmy and I both began to laugh, and then I found that I couldn't stop—not until Clive rubbed my face over with a cloth dipped in cold water. He led me out of the car then, disposing of Jimmy by declaring that I needed medical care. Aunt Esther and Uncle Joe were thus held at bay too, but they both looked worried and upset.

We went along to my compartment and sat down, and Clive handed me a cigarette.

I smoked in silence for a while and then asked abruptly, "what sort of a—what was she killed with? Cleo?"

"Cleo," he repeated. And I said stubbornly, "I'm sure she was Cleo. I think she tore my picture out of that passport and pasted her own in."

He was silent for a moment—not peacefully silent, but in some sort of conflict, and then he asked, "Why?"

"Well, look," I began eagerly. "She was scared of Jimmy—knew that he had seen her killing her uncle—and she figured she'd be me while she got her breath and thought things over. Maybe she was planning to get rid of Jimmy—something like that."

He rested his head against the back of the seat and eyed the overhead light fixture. I watched him until the silence became menacing, and then I asked desperately, "You don't think so?"

"No—I don't. I think you're Cleo. I think your memories are foolery you because you don't want to be Cleo. But I don't believe you killed your uncle—all that stuff is probably some dark scheme of Jimmy's." He got up from the seat, moved restlessly around the confined space, and at last leaned up against the door with his hands in his pockets.

But I wasn't Cleo. I thought I was Virginia Peters, secretary to Old John, who lived in an apartment on Macquarrie Street, in Sydney. It overlooked the Botanical Gardens.

I glanced up at Clive and thought at first that there was something unfriendly in his face, and then decided that he was just worried and unhappy.

He stirred and said flatly, "You'd better be Cleo'"

"But why, for heaven's sake?"

He came and sat down beside me again, frowning and somehow withdrawn.

"Mavis was Cleo," I said firmly, "but she wanted me to think that I was Cleo—she even mentioned having seen me in the movies with the freckle on my chin. I have the freckle, all right, but I have never been in the movies."

He shook his head in an irritated sort of way and rubbed his hand across his forehead, but he did not say anything.

"What's the matter with Virginia Peters?" I asked in sudden fear. "Has she done something dreadful too?"

"No, no—that is, I don't know. But there's one thing I can't understand, and that's why Mavis rushed to catch this train, damaged arm and all. I saw that her arm was taped up, under those flowing sleeves, when she dipped one of them in the soup—and that's why I made that appointment with her in the lounge car. I knew she'd come."

"Hmm," I murmured. "It's wonderful what a nice figure will do for a man."

"Never mind that. You know as well as I do that Mavis would keep that sort of appointment if the man were snowed in with white whiskers."

"Maybe you'd better grow some. I hear she never turned up."

"She was on her way, obviously, when she was lured into your compartment and killed."

I sighed and asked after a moment, "What was used? What weapon? Or is it a secret?"

"Well—Cronlin's found no special weapon, but it looks as though it had been a razor. There are seven men in your carriage, and believe it or not, not one of them uses a safety razor—they all have the old-fashioned lethal weapon."

"What do you use?" I asked abruptly.

He seemed somewhat taken aback, and after giving me a rather cold look he said stiffly, "I don't use a safety either."

I laughed. "Now you know how I feel when you insist that I'm Cleo."

He slumped down in the seat and scowled at the floor.

"Have you just been talking with Cronlin?" I asked.

He nodded.

"You told him about me?"

"Yes. Thought it would be wiser."

"I suppose so," I agreed. "What did he say?"

Clive took a long breath and continued to study the floor. "Perhaps I shouldn't have said anything—but I was afraid it would come out anyway, and it makes a better impression to offer information freely. I told him that, as the only doctor on board, I was giving you medical care until you reached Perth. I said nothing about Jimmy and his accusations."

"Well?"

Clive hesitated, took another long breath, and gave it to me straight.

"Cronlin says that you are Virginia Peters and that you killed Cleo in order to get at her money."

Chapter Nineteen
DOUBLE IDENTITY

I STARED OUT OF THE WINDOW, with my mind almost blank. More of the saltbush and bluebush—only I liked them now. I'd like to be wandering around among them, instead of being penned up in this train like an animal in a trap.

I jerked my head around to Clive and said shrilly, "Cronlin's crazy. How could he possibly think—"

"I'll tell you what he thinks," Clive interrupted. "You and Mavis— who was Cleo at that time—were on the train nearing Albury. Mavis was a talker—as we know—and she gabbed to you about how she was going to meet her relatives, whom she'd never seen, and a fiance who was also a stranger."

"Very odd, that last bit."

"Well. I had to explain why you and I were engaged without ever having seen each other before. I merely told the truth—said Cleo had received a couple of letters from Jimmy which made her think he was going to be a nuisance. I was about to make the same trip, so Bill suggested I pretend to be engaged to Cleo, in order to hold Jimmy off."

"Very feeble," I said coldly. "Why couldn't Cleo simply have announced to the family that she and Bill were engaged?"

Clive grinned faintly and shook his head. "Not until Bill gets his divorce. I had to explain that Cleo and Bill were in love, but—poor Bill—"

"Oh, nuts!" I said. "There are people worse off than Bill."

"But if Mavis *is* Cleo—"

"He still has his wife," I said hardily.

Clive shrugged. "Anyway, Cronlin figured that when the accident happened Cleo was knocked unconscious, and while she lay there you slipped a snapshot of yourself into Cleo's purse, then found that photograph of Cleo and pasted it into your own passport. Apparently there's no doubt about the passport having been tampered with. After completing those arrangements, you pretended to be unconscious yourself—having luckily acquired a nice fat bump on the head to bear you out.

"And why did I tell you that I had lost my memory?"

"To protect yourself in case Cleo was not dead."

"Oh, don't be silly," I said crossly. "How could I think she was dead, when she'd merely strained her arm?"

"She was unconscious, remember, and as a matter of fact, we discovered that she had a head wound. Cronlin thinks—"

"I know what he thinks. That I hit her over the head to finish her off."

"That's the story," Clive agreed, as though relieved to get it off his chest. "Cronlin would be in a frightful wax if he knew I'd told you."

He pulled out a cigarette and handed me one, and I asked slowly, "Why hasn't he arrested me?"

"He couldn't, in any case. He's South Australia mounted police, and we're in Western Australia now. He can't make an arrest here."

"Then we're merely waiting for a Western Australia cop to show up, so that I can be taken into custody?"

"Well, as to that," he said uncertainly, "I don't believe the Western Australia police could arrest you for a crime committed in South Australia. I think they'd have to get authority from South Australia—or something. I'm not quite clear. All I know is that Cronlin has been sending telegrams to all points of the compass, and my private opinion is that they're a bit uncertain about the correct procedure."

I started to laugh and then found that I was crying instead. Clive sat silent beside me—and what could he say, anyway? I thought bitterly. If he used his head, he was bound to think as Cronlin did.

He let me cry for a while and then he handed me a handkerchief and said, "You must try and remember the names of some of your relatives or friends, so that you can get in touch with them at once. Come on now—make an effort. Can't you give me just one name? And I'll telegraph at once."

"I can't," I said despairingly. "I never can, when I try. But I know I've been working for a man in Sydney, and I call him Old John. He's a naturalist, or something of that sort, interested in animals and flowers. We live on Macquarrie Street, in an apartment that overlooks the Botanical Gardens."

Clive wrote it all down in a notebook. "Flat in Macquarrie Street," he murmured. "Right. I'll get hold of that firm of detectives—the ones who are supposed to be tracking down Virginia Peters. They ought to be able to find him, with all this to go on. If—er—"

"If there is such a person," I supplied miserably.

"You cheer up," he said, smiling down at me. "We're getting into Kitchener, where Cronlin is meeting some beaks coming on the other train from Kalgoorlie. He telegraphed them last night."

"That's very cheering news," I admitted. "I can't think why it doesn't cheer me up."

Clive went out, presumably to spring off the train as soon as it got into Kitchener, and I made my way to the lounge car because I was afraid to sit there alone.

The lounge car was fairly well filled, and there was a lively buzz of conversation. Eileen and Uncle Joe had gone to sleep in their chairs, and no one else took any notice of me. I wondered if they knew that I was supposed to have killed Mavis and was running around loose only because everybody's hands were tied with red tape. I quelled a rising desire to laugh wildly.

Cronlin came into the car, made his way to me, and sat down. He gave me a charming smile and offered me a cigarette, which I refused warily. He talked about the weather, opined that it was a good thing the train was air-conditioned, because it was hot as blazes outside, and offered another charming smile.

I accepted it with reserve, and he presently got down to business.

"Would you consent to come back to Port Pirie on the other train with us? It would simplify the investigation considerably, since you are, of course, the most important witness. It would solve most of our troubles."

It would solve all of his troubles, I thought, eying him coldly. I could see him smiling sweetly and offering me cigarettes until we crossed the border, and then he'd warn me about anything I said being used in evidence and arrest me for a murder that I had not committed.

I composed my features and said mildly, "I'm sorry. I have planned to spend Christmas in Perth with my family, and I could not go back now. Later, perhaps."

The sunny good nature left his face, and he asked grimly, "Who are your family?"

I frowned down at my hands. He knew about me, of course—Clive had told him. "I don't know," I said reasonably, "but the Ballisters are nice people, and I think I'd have a merrier Christmas with them than all alone at Port Pirie."

"Don't you think they should be told?"

"Well, yes," I admitted. "I'm going to tell them. I haven't, before this, because I was hoping they *were* my family."

"You know now that you are Virginia Peters, though."

"I am not certain of anything," I protested. "How can I be?"

The train came to a stop, and Cronlin glanced out of the window, jumped up in a hurry, and disappeared. There was a general movement among the passengers, and Uncle Joe woke up.

"Well, well, 'ere we are." He prodded Eileen. "Wake up, kitten."

"I have not been asleep," said Eileen, still remembering to be a lady.

"Don't tell fibs," Aunt Esther reproved her.

"Come on," Uncle Joe boomed, heaving himself to his feet. "We'll go out and have a look at the other train. Must be 'ere by now."

"Here," said Aunt Esther.

We were supposed to get our hats before we went out into the sun, but nothing would induce me to wear the red hat again, so Uncle Joe loaned me something that he called a cricketer's cap. Eileen declared that it looked simply awful, but I stuck to it grimly, and we all went out onto the plain.

All the passengers seemed to be out there, and I could see Cronlin and Clive talking to three men. One of them was in uniform, but it differed from Cronlin's, and I supposed he was a Western Australia trooper. They were quickly surrounded by a crowd of passengers, who tried frankly to listen, so that the five of them presently pushed their way onto the train—presumably in quest of privacy.

The heat was terrific, and the sun seemed to beat onto my head right through the cricketer's cap. I was considering a return to the train, when Jimmy slipped his arm through mine and drew me aside.

"Let's go and have a look at the view."

"There isn't any view," I said crossly. "Nothing we can't see from the train windows."

"That's where you're wrong. See—"

I looked across to a corrugated-iron-roofed shed and saw an aborigine standing in front of it. His torso was bare, but he wore a pair of trousers tied at the waist with a fragment of a sheet, and a bowler hat was perched on his head—rather high, because his hair seemed to be the upswept type.

"He looks kind of natty," I said. "Maybe you boys ought to copy."

Jimmy shook his head. "We haven't the chests for it."

There were other aborigines about, some of the more enterprising throwing boomerangs and then selling them to the crowd.

Jimmy's voice murmured against my ear, "What an evil temper you must have—and what an exhibition of it—last night."

I turned on him, breathless with fury. "I did not kill that girl," I said fiercely, "and don't you ever again say that I did. I am not Cleo Ballister—I'm Virginia Peters."

"So I heard." He gave me a faint smile. "But I don't believe it."

"Where did you hear it?"

"Cronlin has been asking your relatives questions concerning your identity."

"Listen to this," I sad quietly. "It's the truth. I am Virginia Peters, and poor Mavis was Cleo Ballister."

He repeated almost vaguely, "She was Cleo?" and then, quite suddenly, the color drained out of his face and left it gray and terrified.

Chapter Twenty
FAMILY COUNCIL

"JIMMY!" I SAID SHARPLY, because I was afraid that he was going to faint. "What's the matter?"

He sat down on the ground, as though the strength had gone out of his legs, and whispered through colorless lips, "Oh God! That's it."

I watched him curiously and decided that it wasn't just disappointment over Cleo's death and the end of his hope of getting money through her—there was fear in his face and horror.

I sat down beside him and saw that his color had come back a little, but mottled and-queer looking—and in that overpowering heat he was shivering.

"What is it?" I asked. "Something has hit you—you know something—"

He interrupted me and said almost frantically, "No—no, it's all right. Bit of a dizzy turn—I have them sometimes. I'll be better in a minute."

I didn't believe him, but I knew he wouldn't tell me. Something had hit him suddenly and shocked him profoundly, but I knew there was no use in probing. He was completely withdrawn and hardly conscious of me at all.

I looked around and saw that people were beginning to get back onto the train. Wilfred was tearing up and dawn, trying to round up the family, and probably convinced that we two were lost forever.

I prodded Jimmy and said, "Come on, we'll have to go back."

He rose up at once and helped me to my feet. "It's the heat," he said in a sick voice. "Enough to kill you."

It was, too—but I knew quite well that he had not been conscious of the heat until it slid into his mind as an excuse.

I looked at the train and remembered Aunt Esther telling me that the natives called it the Great Black Kanba—the snake of the Nullarbor. It was apt, too—it looked monstrous in the low bush, with no trees to dwarf it.

Wilfred found us and nervously hurried us on board. When we were safely inside he relaxed enough to tell us that Uncle Joe had called a family conference in his compartment.

We went along to Uncle Joe's compartment and found the family assembled—with the exception of Eileen, who had been put out into the corridor. She was merely waiting, I knew, until we had closed the door, to put her ear against it.

The compartment was pretty crowded, once we had arranged ourselves. Aunt Esther, Mary, and I sat on the seat, Wilfred and Jimmy stood by the door, and Uncle Joe stood in front of the washbasin playing with his great gold watch chain and looking unusually serious.

He cleared his throat and opened the meeting. "Now, young lady, that policeman has been asking us if you were really our niece and cousin. We told him that of course we believed you were—but we don't understand why he should doubt it, so we've called a family council."

I wanted badly to laugh, for some reason, but I swallowed it down and set my face in lines of suitable gravity.

"Have you anything to tell us about all this?" Uncle Joe prodded.

"Yes, I have," I said meekly. "I don't believe now that I am your niece—although I certainly thought so when I met you at Melbourne, or I would not have made the trip with you."

This caused a buzz of discussion, and questions were flung at me from all directions. I felt a flash of sorrow for Eileen, on the other side of the door, who was forced, by circumstances, to remain silent.

Uncle Joe finally roared out that they were all to shut up and that he would 'andle the situation himself. Everyone fell silent except Aunt Esther, who said, "Handle."

"Never mind my blasted education now," Uncle Joe said excitedly. He turned to me and started to quiz, and I answered easily enough until we came to Clive. But Clive had to be explained, and at last I shrugged and said, "I don't know why I was supposed to be engaged to him—and he doesn't either. His friend Bill asked him to do it—and I was to be identified at the Melbourne station by that rather startling costume of gray suit and red hat, shoes, and bag. That's all we know about it, and we've been carrying it through because we supposed that there must be some good reason behind it."

I drew a long breath and felt that I'd been pretty clever. I had not mentioned Jimmy, and so had avoided a family upheaval. Not that Jimmy deserved my protection, but I knew nothing about that supposed murder in Perth, and I felt that it was wiser to remain silent until I did. A quick glance at Jimmy showed me that he looked considerably relaxed and almost normal.

Uncle Joe was toying with his walrus mustache and saying "Shh" to anyone who ventured an opinion.

He presently set the path of procedure for all of them by saying, "I'll have to think this over—but it's lunch time, and we don't want to get indigestion. We'll eat now and discuss things later. As for you, my girl—we'll continue to call you Cleo. You're a likable young woman, and if you aren't our girl, then we can still have you for a friend."

I was touched and said, "Thank you," warmly. "I feel the need for friends right now."

"All right, then," said Uncle Joe, and pounded for the door. "Come on, everybody—lunch."

He flung open the door—just a shade too quickly for Eileen, who almost overbalanced. However, with great presence of mind for one so young, she said, "My goodness, Uncle Joe, you nearly had me over on the floor. I was just going to knock and tell you that it's time for lunch."

"Is it, then?" Uncle Joe laughed, looking at her fondly. "Well, come along, young'un."

He led the way to the diner, and we followed along—a general at the head of his troops.

We met Clive on the way, and he fell in with us. He took my arm and whispered, "Good news, for a change. The Kalgoorlie constabulary think Sergeant Cronlin's analysis of the case is all wrong. They say he makes no explanation as to why Mavis followed on and took an assumed name, and they've decided to do their own investigating. I gather it's just by way of practice, since the investigation rightly belongs to South Australia. Nothing will be done, therefore, until we reach Kalgoorlie."

"I'm glad of a little time," I said, feeling relieved. "What will they do at Kalgoorlie?"

He grinned. "As far as I can make out, they're going to blow the dust off the book of rules and try to find out the correct procedure in a case like this."

I felt comfortably relaxed. Perhaps we'd hear from Old John—or I might find out something about my relatives and my circumstances. I'd have to think—I'd spend the afternoon thinking.

Eileen squeezed past me and trod on my sore feet, and I thought triumphantly that the red shoes most certainly were not mine—they hurt too much.

I was reminded of my glib statement that Clive was to recognize me by my costume, and I asked him about it, but he shook his head. He had been given a description of the family, and was to pick them out at the station and wait near them. It hadn't been easy, either, as he had seen at least three groups that looked like ours.

"Maybe you never did get the right people," I suggested brightly. But he said he'd been given the names, and he doubted whether there was another family with names like the Ballisters.

When we reached the diner Uncle Joe started to direct the seating arrangements, as usual, but Eileen, who was the only one who ever really spoke up to him, made such an uproar about her designated place that she was allowed to mix everything up. In the end Clive and I were seated with Mary and Wilfred, which didn't suit Uncle Joe, because he had wanted to question us. However, the waiter slid a menu under his nose, and he quieted down. Uncle Joe loved menus.

This one was particularly entertaining I thought. I noted an item near the bottom—*Passion fruit and cream,* and could hear Old John's monotonous voice intoning, "We get the passion vine and the beautiful passionflower in some places, but without the fruit, as it is in Australia. Here the fruit is a rare table delicacy—most delectable."

I decided to try it and forego the usual bread, rice, or tapioca pudding. I had been intending to cut out the puddings anyway, because I'd figured that if I didn't, the seams of the gray skirt would give out before we reached Kalgoorlie. I was blindly determined, money or no money, to buy some sort of a new garment at Kalgoorlie.

I wondered, suddenly, whether Mavis had my clothes in her luggage. I could ask permission to try on whatever she had, anyway—and I had a strong conviction that they would fit perfectly.

"Of course I've always lived in or near the city all my life," Mary was saying. "Either at Beaconsfield or right in Perth. In Beaconsfield I always went to the Congregational church, but in Perth we went Presbyterian."

"Lovely place, Perth," I said thoughtlessly.

Mary widened her eyes at me. "But how do you know—if you haven't had your memory?"

"It's what I hear from the mob," I said absently, and then blushed and added, "The people on the train, you know—they all seem to think so."

"My sister says it's very hot," Clive observed. "Now, in Sale—"

"Oh, quiet," I groaned. "I've heard all that I ever want to about Sale."

"But, my dear affianced," he protested reasonably, "we are going to live there after we're married."

Mary and Wilfred gaped, and I said hastily, "Cut it out, Clive—they know all."

"Oh. Well, Sale would be the only place for me if I were married."

"You look out," I said ominously, "or you may be an old maid all your life."

Mary laughed heartily at this, but Wilfred took it all very seriously.

"I think a man should decide where he wants his home, and his wife should follow him."

"Well, I followed you to Perth," Mary admitted, "but if you ever decided to go back to Beaconsfield, you'd have to get behind me and push."

She laughed again, while Wilfred assumed a sulky expression.

"I think a husband and wife should live where they please and just go to visit each other occasionally," I said.

They all disagreed with me violently, and Mary pointed out, "The children need a father's influence."

"Oh well, that's all right," I conceded. "The children could remain with the father. That would make it easier for the wife, anyway."

There was an appalled silence, and Wilfred stopped a forkful of food midway between the table and his mouth. I heard a strangled noise from the table across the aisle and looked up to find Uncle Joe regarding me with horror and reproof.

"Now, look 'ere, young woman—that'll be about enough of that. A mother and her children—" But the rest was lost to me, as several men passed along the aisle between our tables and blocked off our view of each other.

I glanced up and saw that they were what Clive had called the Western Australia constabulary. Cronlin was following them, and when he came to my table he paused and looked down at me.

"Miss Peters, why didn't you tell me that you and Cleo Ballister had been friends for some time before you started on that trip from Sydney?"

Chapter Twenty-One
VIRGINIA PETERS'S CLOTHES

I DIDN'T TELL YOU that Cleo Ballister was an old friend of mine for the very good reason that I didn't know it," I said to Cronlin, in sudden fury. "I've told you that I've lost my memory—and I'll thank you to hand over any other information that you've found out about me."

Cronlin frowned, and the Western Australia contingent grinned fleetingly. One of them cleared his throat and murmured, "Plenty of time later, Sergeant."

"I said she was a friend the first time I saw her on this train," I went on, calming down a bit, "only I didn't really know it then. But she'd changed the color of her hair—must have blonded it on the train."

"I'm afraid I don't quite follow," Mary said, her eyes shifting eagerly from me to the retreating policemen. Wilfred was gaping at me, with his loaded fork again stalled in midair. I resisted an impulse to flip it neatly over into Uncle Joe's soup—I was sure I could do it—and said instead, "Eat your lunch, Wilfred, and stop playing with it."

Mary gave me an evil look, and from across the aisle Uncle Joe bellowed, "I'll be blowed if I can see why we should all be tied up in this. We're decent, quiet people, on our way 'ome."

"Home."

I heard Jimmy give a quick sigh, and he said in a low voice, "I wish we were there now." I glanced at him and decided that he looked far from happy.

Mary murmured under her breath, "Fancy Uncle Joe calling himself a quiet person."

She giggled, and Wilfred said, "Still," and looked quickly over at Uncle Joe.

"I wish I could get hold of that passport," I said to Clive.

"What passport?"

"Mine. My Virginia Peters passport. I'd like to know how old I am and what my occupation is. Did you happen to look?"

Clive shook his head. "I didn't have much time, you know."

"What's this?" Mary asked inquisitively.

"I wish I'd looked at the contents of that pocketbook," I mourned. "It might have helped. We were in too much of a hurry."

Clive said, "I suppose so," and I added, "Do you think they'd let us look now?"

"Hardly. I'm afraid you'll just have to wait."

"What *are you* talking about?" Mary asked.

I frowned down at my plate and thought, *But I don't want to wait— I don't see why the police should have all the ammunition on their side.* I wondered where they were keeping all Mavis's stuff—big things like the suitcases—and decided that they probably were locked into the compartment in which she had been murdered.

"Our next stop," said Wilfred, consulting his watch, "is at Zanthus, at one forty-five. In about half an hour."

Mary remarked, "You'd think they'd be afraid that the lunatic who killed that poor girl would get off the train at one of these stops and just run."

Clive, stirring his tea, glanced out over the plain and said, "Where could he run to? He'd be picked up in a couple of hours at the outside by the mounted police—with the help of one or two black trackers."

"Those black trackers," said Wilfred, preparing to give a little lecture, "aborigines, you know, are extraordinarily clever at tracking a fugitive. I understand that they—"

"Hasn't Uncle Joe finished?" I asked restlessly, and only vaguely conscious that I was interrupting Wilfred. "I want to go—but I know that one does not depart before the king."

Mary giggled, and I was astounded to see the faintest flicker of a smile on Wilfred's face before he quickly wiped it off.

"What's the matter with you?" Clive asked. "You haven't had your sweet yet."

"Oh," I said. "The passion fruit. I'd forgotten."

As a matter of fact, the passion fruit turned out to be as delicious as advertised. Clive advanced the theory that the passion fruit of Sale was a cut above any other kind, but I said, "This is quite good enough for me. I don't need to live in Sale to get it any better."

I had barely finished, when Uncle Joe swept his walrus with a napkin and rose to his feet, and we all rose after him and followed him from the diner.

"I'm going to me compartment for a bit of a rest," he threw over his shoulder. "I'm still feeling dicky after that attack last night."

"Good," said Aunt Esther; "Jimmy, you ought to go and lie down too. You re not looking quite the thing."

"Oh, let me alone," Jimmy muttered irritably. "I'm perfectly all right."

Aunt Esther folded her lips, but Uncle Joe barked, "All right, boy—keep your blasted shirt on."

Eileen, skipping around among us, inadvertently tripped Uncle Joe at that point, and he thudded over against a window. He gave her a box on the ear, and she dissolved into tears.

"It was an accident, Uncle Joe—she didn't mean to trip you," Mary said defensively. "You needn't have hit her." She put her arm around Eileen, who wailed a bit louder.

Uncle Joe made no reply and plodded on doggedly. Clive and Jimmy dropped off at their own compartments, and when we reached our car the rest of us separated with hardly a word.

In our compartment Aunt Esther started to arrange herself in the corner with a pillow, but I made her stretch out on the seat.

"I'll take the floor," I said firmly. "I can't be bothered getting that top bunk down—and anyway, we'll be at that place Zanthus soon, and I want to get off. After that I'm going to the lounge car."

She went off to sleep almost at once, and I sat on the floor and smoked a couple of cigarettes. My memory was moving sluggishly, but I was still very much confused, and it was infuriating to think that the police had information about me that they would not disclose. I made up my mind to go to them, immediately after the Zanthus stop, and see if I could make them open up.

I tried to concentrate for a while on my defective memory, but the only thing that I brought into the light was a picture of myself on the steamer, washing my hands, with the soap slithering away. And of what use was that?

My mind went back to the Ballisters. Uncle Joe hadn't painted a masterpiece today that had been finished by some rank amateur. And Jimmy—what was the matter with him? He had become quiet and seemed very nervous. I thought he was afraid too—but what could he be afraid of? Something in his mind, that he had thought up.

Mavis had been scared too—she must have been, or why had she changed her name and her hair? And why on earth had she followed me in such a hurry? She'd had something to be scared of, of course—unless there was a mistake, and it should have been Aunt Esther or myself lying in that berth with a gaping throat.

No, I thought, *that isn't right.* Mavis wouldn't be lying in Aunt Esther's berth. She had been enticed into our compartment, probably while she was on her way to the appointment with Clive. She'd met someone in the corridor of this car while I was in the lounge hunting Uncle Joe's lizard. Jimmy had been out there with me for a while, but he'd gone back when Clive had come. Clive couldn't have done it, then—he'd been with me—and Aunt Esther, Uncle Joe, and Wilfred had all been together. Mary and Eileen had been sleeping.

I thought of the little lizard that had been in our compartment for so long, and then, after Mavis had been murdered, it must have run across her body and so tracked blood out into the corridor.

I shuddered and then started violently as someone rapped an the door.

It turned out to be the four policemen, and I came out into the corridor and closed the door behind me.

"My aunt is sleeping in there," I explained, looking them over.

"It was you we wanted," Cronlin said ambiguously. He held up a suitcase and added, "Some of your clothes. We'd like you to try them on—see if they fit."

I almost snatched the bag and said eagerly "Yes, of course." I backed into the compartment and shut the door in their faces.

As soon as I had raised the lid of the suitcase I knew that the clothes were mine—there was no doubt about it whatever. I could even remember buying one of the dresses, a brown-and-white print that was very simple and very smart, and I had not bought it in Australia, but in New York. I put it on with hands that were actually trembling and then tried to see as much of myself as I could in the small mirror. Oh yes, the dress was mine, and the fit perfect. I felt a refreshing flow of confidence. I knew who I was now, and they could accuse me or not as they liked, but I'd fight.

Aunt Esther had not moved, and I tiptoed back into the corridor, anxious not to disturb her. I knew that she had not had much sleep the night before and that she must be very tired.

The constabulary surveyed me—admiringly, I thought.

"You see," I said, pivoting, "I am Virginia Peters. I wish you'd tell me what you know about me. I can remember some things, but it would make such a big difference if you'd help me out."

There was a short silence, and then one of them spoke up. "Miss Peters—I suppose you *are* Miss Peters—we'll have more information at Zanthus. But there's one thing we must turn up, and that's Cleo Ballister's passport."

"I don't have it," I protested. "It wasn't in her bag. The only thing to identify her was an application for a driver's license."

They looked at each other, and one of them said to Cronlin, "If that is so, then she could have lost her memory and thought she was the other one. Without a picture, you see—"

Cronlin closed up his mouth and looked sulky, and the man turned to me and said politely, "Can't you remember anything about your association with Cleo Ballister in Sydney? The two of you were friends there."

I looked at them blankly and then thought of Mavis, but I couldn't picture her with brown hair—there was no response from my mind.

Cronlin shifted his great body and spoke curtly.

"I've tried to tell you before, but you won't listen to me. It's Miss Peters's passport—it must have been there in her bag at the time of the accident at Albury—and it evidently had Miss Ballister's picture pasted in it then, or the two of them would not have been identified as they were."

Chapter Twenty-Two
ODD TELEGRAM

THERE WAS A SILENCE after Cronlin had spoken, and I thought wildly that of course he was right. How could they have identified us as they did, if my photograph had been in my passport? Mavis's photograph must have been pasted in there even then. By whom? I wasn't Cleo—it was definitely established, now, that I was Virginia Peters—but I seemed to have been up to some sort of mischief, anyway. One or both of us must have tampered with the passport.

"What about it, Miss Peters?" the detective asked while Cronlin kept a cold, calculating eye on me.

I put my hands to my head and said wearily, "I don't know. It sounds as though you must be right, but I don't know anything about it—except that I *couldn't* be a party to a thing like that."

Cronlin spoke again. "The Ballister girl could hardly have done it all by herself—she'd need your cooperation. She couldn't know that you were going to lose your memory—if you did."

"Now, then, Sergeant," said the detective reprovingly. He peered out of the window and added, "Well, here we are at Zanthus. Come on, boys. Talk with you later, Miss Peters."

They clattered off the train and left me there in the corridor, feeling furious. I wanted so badly to remember things, and so much had come back to me, yet I could not recall being friends with Mavis in Sydney.

The door of Uncle Joe's compartment burst open, and he emerged with his arms full of paints, a watercolor block, and various other things. Wilfred followed, looked harassed and unhappy and bearing an easel.

Uncle Joe nodded to me and said cheerfully, " 'Ullo. Come on out, girl, and stretch your legs. I'm going to make a sketch of the landscipe."

He banged past me, and Wilfred trailed after him, saying futilely, "You won't have time—I know there isn't time. You might lose some of your materials—we might not be able to get them back onto the train in time."

I followed them out and found that Zanthus was just another Nullarbor station—a few small buildings with corrugated iron roofs and flat desert landscape. Uncle Joe, with a flood of confusing instructions to Wilfred, set up his easel and began to sketch with scarcely a glance at the scene before him. There was no aborigine in sight, but as I watched the block under Uncle Joe's swift strokes, an aborigine, with arm extended, became the central figure. Various bits of the bush soon appeared behind him, and in a few seconds a train materialized in the distance. Uncle Joe turned to beam up at me.

"See? The Great Black Kanba bearing down on him."

"Kanba means snake," Wilfred explained proudly. "The great kanba of the Nullarbor. The blacks thought that the first train through the Nullarbor was the return of the huge legendary snake which had been wounded and run off the plain by two Abos many years ago and—"

"You save your ruddy lectures," said Uncle Joe, "for when they're wanted. I'm going to call this picture The Great Black Kanba. It's shaping up to look like the best thing I've done."

Wilfred became silent and fell to studying the horizon, and I wandered off to join Mary and Eileen, who had just descended from the lounge car. Aunt Esther had not appeared, and I wondered whether I should have wakened her. She might have liked to get off the train for a breathing spell, I thought—and then decided that you couldn't breathe much, anyway, because it was too hot. I realized that I had no hat and hastily covered my head with my hands.

Eileen ran to meet me and began to exclaim over my dress. "Oh, you do look so nice. Where did you get it? Why didn't you put it on before?"

"I'd forgotten that I had it."

"I don't see how you could forget a pretty frock like that," said the kid. "Why have you got your hands on your head?"

"To keep my hair from blowing away."

I could not see the police anywhere, and Clive had not appeared either. I wondered which one of the buildings was the telegraph office and what was happening there.

"You look very silly standing there with your hands on your head like that," Eileen mentioned.

I saw Jimmy standing by himself, and he caught my eye and turned away. Not in love with me any more, apparently. He knew that I was not Cleo now, and he felt himself in trouble because I might tell on him, especially since Cleo's death. Perhaps he was contemplating steps to silence me. I shivered a little in the broiling sun—Cleo had been silenced. But Jimmy had not done that—he had thought I'd done it at first, and now he suspected someone else, and he was frightened. I was frightened too, I thought tiredly, and confused.

"—about Christmas, you see, because Christmas is only next week, and then on Boxing Day we're all going to Cottesloe Beach for our picnic."

I focused my attention on the kid and asked in mild surprise, "You mean you're going out for a picnic on Christmas Day?"

"Oh *no,* not on *Christmas*—we're going on Boxing Day, the day after Christmas. On Christmas we'll get our presents and have our dinner, and the plum pudding will have money in it and a button and a ring—only I hope I don't get the buttons because that means you're going to be an old maid, but if you get the ring, you'll be married next. I hope," said the child, "I get most of the money."

I thought of Christmas at home in New York with my father. Last Christmas—and then he had died in April. I felt some of that recent grief, and yet I could not picture him clearly. My mother? No—there was no remembrance of her at all. But I did remember my home—an apartment, pleasant and comfortable, with Father there. After he died Aunt Shep came and took me back with her to Los Angeles, and then Old John—Osborne, that was it—John Osborne had employed me, the puttering old ruddy. I laughed. He was nice, though—he had been nice to me. I'd come out to Australia with him.

I began to feel dizzy and light-headed under such a rush of memory. It was too much, all at once. Somebody caught me by the arm and began to hustle me onto the train. It was Clive, and he said, "What did I tell you about keeping that already defective head of yours covered? Anyway, do you want to get left behind? We're about to leave."

We jostled the conductor, who was carrying Uncle Joe's easel, and as we got on board we jostled Uncle Joe, who was reaching out for the easel. We missed Wilfred, who was carefully handling the newly painted picture.

"Got a day's work in there," Uncle Joe announced happily. "Got the feel of the thing. If any ruddy fool tries to finish this one for me—"

I didn't hear what evil fate was in store for the mischievous amateur as Clive steered me away.

"There was a telegram for you," he said in a low voice, "but the police intercepted it. I suppose they'll give it to you after they've had it under the magnifying glass."

I sighed and asked after a minute, "It was addressed to Virginia Peters?"

Clive nodded. "It seemed to puzzle them a bit. They read it over about six times, looked at it from every angle, and then told me it wouldn't interest me, as I was on the medical side of the case, when I tried to look over their shoulders."

"I wish they'd give it to me," I said forlornly. "Maybe it's from someone who belongs to me. I'd like to have some sort of a definite link with—with somebody. Where are we going?"

"Lounge car, of course—for afternoon tea."

"But it's barely two o'clock."

"Even so," said Clive comfortably, "that leaves only two hours to wait. I like your frock—where did you get it?"

"The cops let me try it on, and if they'd wanted it back they'd have had to tear it off me."

"I'm glad to see that your taste is fairly quiet," he grinned. "The ladies of Sale abhor vulgarity."

"I'll send an advance telegram of apology for what I've been wearing the last couple of days."

"Quite unnecessary," he assured me. "I'll keep your secret and they'll never know."

"Cheating," I said, "ill becomes a son of Sale."

The lounge car was deserted, and I asked, "Where is everybody?"

"Packing, probably."

"Packing? Why?"

"We'll be in at Kalgoorlie at five-twenty."

"Do you seriously mean that we have to change trains again?" I asked, astounded.

"At Kalgoorlie. We take the regular Western Australia railway system there. Different gauge from this—three foot six, to be exact—but they say it rides fairly comfortably."

"Next time I cross Australia," I said feebly, "I'll use a bicycle."

"Suit yourself."

"Come off it, Doctor. If I have to apologize to the ladies of Sale for my red hat, the least you can do is to feel slightly ashamed at the stubbornness of the Australia Rylway System."

"All I feel," he said, "is a desire to slap your ears back."

"Maybe it would help. Anyway, don't bother me—I want to think. I have almost my entire life at my fingertips— all but a little bit—the bit in Sydney. I can't remember what I was doing in Sydney for the last few months—outside of my work for Old John."

"All right," he said agreeably. "Go ahead and think. I'll play a little soft music for you."

He went to the piano and began to pick out a tune with one finger, but I couldn't identify it because he made so many mistakes. I couldn't think, either, because I kept on trying to make out what he was playing.

The police came pouring in presently, and I looked out of the window, hummed lightly, and tried to appear nonchalant. I noticed out of the corner of my eye, and with satisfaction, that Cronlin had picked up a dirty spot on the fancy white stripe of his trousers.

They surrounded me, and Clive moved up quietly and leaned over the back of my chair. One of them handed me a telegram and asked, "Can you explain this, Miss Peters?"

I was conscious of Clive leaning closer, so that we read the thing together: *Happy birthday, darling. Doctor Butler not rich; don't bother with him. Love, Marge.*

Chapter Twenty-Three
THE MOVING CORPSE

I CLOSED MY EYES for a moment and felt myself blushing furiously. I wanted to say something light and careless that would pass the situation off, but not one solitary word of the right sort presented itself to me. I thought, with a spasm of anger, that even a policeman should have sense enough to keep Clive from reading the wretched telegram.

He straightened up and moved away, but he was the first to speak into that uncomfortable silence.

"The woman lies," he said mildly. "I'm well oiled, as a matter of fact. Dinkum."

Cronlin moved his shoulders impatiently. "Miss Peters, your employer states that he permitted you to take this trip at your own insistence. You gave as a reason that you were not feeling well, and since a friend of yours was about to make the trip, you wanted to travel with her. The friend, of course, was Cleo Ballister. Now, did she tell you, before that accident near Albury, that Doctor Butler was not rich—as you evidently had thought he was?"

I almost laughed. Naive old Cronlin, I thought hysterically. Disappointed in Doctor Butler's supposed fortune, Miss Peters looks about for another way to acquire money and settles on taking the place and identity of her friend. The leftover friend, of course, must be killed to avoid complications.

I stood up and looked Cronlin in the eye. "She didn't tell me a thing—it is really quite a blow. I had it all planned—even to my wedding dress and how I'd spend his money. And now, gentlemen, if you will excuse me, I have to go to the ladies' room.

I made my exit in a shocked and defeated silence. No Australian, I was sure, would follow me after an announcement like that.

I went along to my own compartment with my mind moving confusedly. Marge was a friend of mine, all right—an Australian girl, lively

118

and talkative—and I thought that I remembered her with Cleo. Cleo and Marge and I having tea somewhere and laughing—always laughing.

It must be my birthday—and so it was, of course—just before Christmas. The nineteenth of December—no, the twentieth—Marge was a day early with her greetings.

Cleo must have told us about Clive, and Marge decided to get funny about him. Only it wasn't funny—it was awful. I felt my face begin to burn again.

Aunt Esther was still stretched out on the seat sleeping, and there was no convenient place for me to sit. I moved over to the window and looked out. Still the saltbush plain, and I noticed white streaks on the ground, stretching out between the bushes like bleaching bones.

I began to think about my passport and to wonder why the people on the train near Albury had not found it and identified me properly. I felt certain that Cleo could not have had her picture in it then. What was she doing, anyhow, sticking her picture into my passport? When did she find out I had lost my memory, so that she knew she could take my place? And she had blonded her hair. But Cleo was always changing the color of her hair. That brown hair was dyed too—she had told me. Said she had to visit her relatives, and she thought it was policy to lie a bit quiet and refined. That application in her pocketbook described her as having brown hair and blue eyes—the one that had identified me.

But how did she know that I had lost my memory? She had hurried on to Melbourne, in time to catch the train for Adelaide, and then, I thought, she had approached me and had seen very quickly that there was something wrong with me—and so she had hung around and observed us. Relieved, probably, that I had taken her place, because it had become a bit too hot, and she was scared. Jimmy was threatening, for one thing.

So in Adelaide she had bought her favorite bleach and fixed her hair up so that it felt natural again and so that it matched the picture which she proceeded to paste into my passport.

She started to make up to Clive next, and to her family. And then one of them killed her. But perhaps they thought they were killing me! I looked at the closed door of the compartment and had a moment of absolute terror.

No. It was no use thinking that way—I'd have to refute Cronlin's stupid theory. But I'd need to find out why my passport had not been found at Albury to identify me. I thought of my suitcase, and a quick glance around confirmed my suspicion that the police had taken it away again. But it seemed probable to me that I had kept my passport in the suitcase, because the navy-blue pocketbook had been a bit small for it. I thought for a moment and then remembered. There was an extra flap pocket right at the bottom of that suitcase, and I had kept all my important papers there. It was not a secret pocket that anybody would be sure to find, but something that the people at Albury could easily have overlooked.

I felt that I must look in that pocket—I simply had to. I supposed that the suitcase was locked in my old compartment, but the doors did not lock very well from the outside, and perhaps I'd be able to get in.

I slipped out of the compartment and went quietly along the corridor. I could hear the door rattling before I got there, and when I examined it I saw that the lock had been turned but had not caught properly. I had only to push and maneuver the door a little, and it swung open.

I went in, closed the door behind me, and then was suddenly and badly shocked to discover that the sheeted body still lay along the seat. I nearly turned and fled, but I had caught sight of my suitcase, and the urge to look at my papers was very strong. The shade was drawn, and in the semi-gloom I crept to where my suitcase stood on the floor and dropped down in front of it. I fumbled nervously with the fastenings and at last got them open and the lid pushed back.

The pocket was at the bottom, all right, and I pulled a bundle of papers out of it. It was too dark to see properly, so I cautiously raised the shade a little to get a better light.

The plain slid by outside—bare and dreary, without beginning and without end—but I turned away from it and began to riffle through the papers. There should be something there, I thought, that would clear the last mists away from my identity. I knew so much now, and yet a little thing like Marge's telegram was still inexplicable. I wanted desperately to take the papers and run back to my compartment, but I was afraid of getting into trouble.

There was a sound, muffled and unfamiliar, and I looked in sweating terror at the sheeted figure, but it was quiet and still. Fear pulled me to my feet and halfway to the door, and then I set my jaw and turned back. I snatched up one of the papers, a bill for a purse. I threw it down and then came across a letter. It was from Aunt Shep, and I glanced through it quickly. Aunt Shep's doings— she went here and there and did this and that. She hoped I was all right and wished that I were not so far away. I thrust it aside and picked up a bankbook. It was a Sydney bank, and I had a balance of forty-two pounds, three shillings, and tenpence. Not bad—much better than Cleo's bank account. There was a letter of introduction to some people in Perth—a very nice letter signed by Alice Hayworth. Who was she? Oh yes—people living out in Wahroonga, on Sydney's north shore. Nice house, they had—and a beautiful flower garden. I remembered vividly the combined scent of all those flowers—and suddenly I was staring at the still figure stretched along the seat. There was no odor of death. But of course it was cool—that was why they had left her instead of taking her along to the baggage car.

I turned determinedly to the papers again. The passport was there but I threw it aside and picked up some more letters. There were some from friends at home, and then one from Marge, from the Blue Mountains in Australia. She was on a vacation and said, *Cleo and I are having a bonzer time, but the men are scarce. Cleo has gone off the deep end with a man named Bill. No money, and he has a wife! Just like Cleo, of course—but she says she has other means of getting money. A bunch of boring relatives. I told her it's been my experience that you don't get money out of relatives, boring or otherwise, but she merely said wait and see.*

I folded the letter and began to put all the papers away. I hadn't really learned anything that I did not know, and I couldn't stay in that terrifying place any longer. I closed the suitcase and pulled the shade down again.

As I turned to go I looked at the figure under its white shroud and was suddenly frozen rigid. I thought that the sheet had moved slightly.

But that was impossible, I told myself feverishly—she'd been dead since last night. I measured the distance from where I stood to the door with my eyes and wondered wildly how I could possibly make it. I drew a steadying breath. It was stupid to be afraid of a corpse, and I had seen with my own eyes that Cleo was dead.

I took a step forward and got no farther. This time there was no doubt about it—the body under the sheet was moving.

Chapter Twenty-Four
MURDER IS SERIOUS

THE HEAD WAS MOVING, and it turned toward me—and I could not stir—
I couldn't even scream. The sheet slipped down, and I saw black hair
and then dark eyes, blank and dull. There was blood on the chin.

I whispered, "Jimmy!" and I think he became conscious of me just
for a moment. The eyes lost their glazed opacity, and he muttered, "The
carpenter." There was a brief struggle, and the words "toggle bolt" came
out quite clearly. He seemed to go away after that. The eyes half closed
and went out like snuffed candles, and the mouth sagged open.

I stumbled frantically to the door, wrenched it open, and half fell
into the corridor. There was no one in sight, and I made my way down
to my own compartment on shaking legs and with my breath coming in
short, quick gasps. I had some vague idea of rousing Aunt Esther and
getting her help, but when I pushed open the door I saw that she was
up longer there. I stood there for a moment, looking helplessly at the
empty seat—and then I heard footsteps and voices and knew that it was
the police.

I slipped into the compartment, closed the door, and leaned against
it, still panting. They'd surely stop at that other compartment and go
in—and then I wouldn't have to tell them and admit that I'd been there.
They'd arrest me if they knew—I was sure of it. If they didn't go in
there, I'd have to tell someone, though—because Jimmy wasn't dead.

They stopped, and I heard the door rattle and drew a great, gasping breath of relief. There was a short period of indefinite sounds, and
then one of them was out in the corridor again, calling sharply for the
conductor. I moved over and fell onto the seat, with my head on Aunt
Esther's pillow. My exhausted mind went blank for a while, and then I
found myself thinking that when they came to question me I'd tell them
that I'd been sleeping. I even tried to sleep, but my mind was talking so
loudly by then that it kept me awake. I tried not to listen, and found

that my ears were straining for the faintest sound from out in the corridor.

I should have gone to meet them and told them, I thought hysterically. They'd surely find out that I had been there, and then things would look ten times worse for me. But it was too late now—I'd have to stick to what I'd done.

I hadn't long to wait. One of them came along almost immediately and walked right in, with only the suggestion of a prefacing knock.

It seemed that he was Sergeant Detective Brewster, and as I pretended to emerge from sleep he said, "I want an account of your movements, miss, since you left the lounge car about half an hour ago."

I closed my eyes, yawned, shook my head, and opened them again.

"Miss Peters," said Brewster, still courteous, but with a faint hint of menace, "I'm waiting."

The best defense is attack, I thought, and sat straight up and glared at him.

"You had no right whatever," I said sharply, "to let Doctor Butler see that telegram. It was only sent as a joke, obviously, but it was extremely embarrassing for me that he should have read it. You could certainly have picked a more opportune time to show it to me and ask me about it. I want to cooperate with you, of course—but blunders like that are discouraging, to say the least."

There was only the faintest change in his expression, and he said with impersonal courtesy, "I'm sorry, but murder is serious, and we wanted Doctor Butler's reaction to that telegram."

"What were his reactions?" I asked coldly.

"Miss Peters, we are getting away from the point. I want an account of your movements since you left us in the lounge car."

I no longer had to simulate anger—I actually felt it. "I walked through several cars," I said hotly "blushing all over. When I came to this compartment I looked in, but my Aunt Esther was sleeping here, and I didn't want to disturb her. I walked on through some more cars, until I came to the diner, and then I turned back. I looked out a window in one of the corridors and smoked a cigarette. And then I smoked another one."

"In the corridor of one of the carriages up ahead?"

"Yes," I said defiantly, "and then I came back here. Aunt Esther had gone, so I lay down and had a sleep."

"All right, miss. Would you mind showing me the spot where you stood and smoked the two cigarettes?"

I got up slowly, with a hollow feeling somewhere inside me. Why had I been such a fool as to mention smoking? He wanted to see the butts and ashes, of course—there'd have been nowhere to put them but on the floor. And there wouldn't be any butts or ashes.

We went out into the corridor, and I walked as slowly as I dared. I asked, and hoped it sounded idle, "Why are you so anxious to know what I've been doing?"

Brewster made no reply, and my palms and forehead came out in a cold sweat. What of Jimmy? Was he still living? I hoped desperately that he was, and that he could tell them I had never harmed him.

I walked through one car with the policeman padding grimly behind me. It had to be the next car, because the one after that was the diner. I'd have to pick a spot and stick to it—and suggest that someone had cleaned the debris away. And then Brewster would summon the attendants, and they would deny having cleaned up any stubs or ashes. But I had a stroke of luck, and it seemed to me the first bit of luck I'd had for years. Halfway up that last corridor, on the floor, I saw a messy little area of two cigarette butts and some scattered ash.

I averted my eyes hastily and pretended not to notice it. "It was up there somewhere," I said with a vague wave of my hand.

Brewster went on ahead of me and stooped and picked up the butts. "These yours?" he asked pleasantly.

I glanced at them indifferently and said, "I don't know."

He turned the messy, crumbling things over in his fingers. "Just what kind of cigarette do you smoke?"

My mind leaped and began to move around like a squirrel in a cage. What could I say? Those butts would never be the same brand as the cigarettes I'd been smoking.

"I don't know," I said uncertainly. "I've been trying to get used to the Australian cigarettes, and I'm smoking all kinds now."

He nodded rather woodenly and put the two stubs into an envelope while I looked on and thought foolishly that policemen certainly had to do some dirty jobs, at times, and really earned their money.

He motioned me to go back down the corridor, and we returned to my car. There were some people milling around by now, and I saw Aunt Esther crying into a handkerchief, while Uncle Joe patted her shoulder. Wilfred stood with them, looking distressed. He caught sight of me and hurried over, his mouth working excitedly. "A terrible thing has happened. Dreadful, dreadful! Someone has murdered Jimmy!"

"He's—dead?" I gasped.

"Yes, yes—Doctor Butler told us. He is in there now."

I turned away, feeling sick and seared and brushed past Brewster, who was right behind me. I went into my compartment and sat down by the window. I stared out at the landscape with dull eyes, until suddenly, and with a sense of shock, I saw a tree—just one tree, growing by itself, serene and lovely. I twisted my cold hands together and watched avidly, and presently I saw two more trees, growing together in friendly proximity. I drew a free little breath and thought numbly, *We're off the plain, anyway—no matter what's going to happen.*

I opened up Cleo's great red pocketbook and was conscious of a spasm of annoyance. They ought to give me my own things, so that I could have a purse to match my brown dress. It was absurd for me to be using Cleo's things. Cleo was dead.

My face, in the little pocket mirror, looked dreadful—pale and haggard, with great dark smudges under the eyes. I powdered my nose, put a little color on my lips and combed my hair, but somehow it didn't seem to make much difference.

Poor Jimmy—he had been frightened, and he knew what was going on—but he wouldn't tell. He should have told the police—he'd still be alive if he had. But perhaps he had not been sure, and it was possible, too, that he had considered blackmail. I'd have to tell the police about him, if only to protect myself—and that would mean casting a slur on Cleo. I hated to do that, because I liked Cleo. Only how could I like a person of that sort?

Aunt Esther came in with Uncle Joe supporting her and Wilfred hovering helplessly in the background.

" 'Ere we are, then," said Uncle Joe as I stood up. We made Aunt Esther lie down, and I arranged the pillow under her head.

"Easy does it," said Uncle Joe gently. "Just you lie quiet there, Es, and we'll 'ave a cup of tea in a jiff."

Aunt Esther looked at the ceiling through a film of tears. "I told Madge I'd take care of him—I promised her. And I haven't done it, or he wouldn't be lying there like that."

"Hush, Mother," Wilfred said, patting her hand. "You know you did your best for Jimmy. You did all that was humanly possible."

"Oh no, no," she moaned, and moved her head from side to side on the pillow. Wilfred knelt beside her, and Uncle Joe stood breathing noisily and shaking his head. I slipped out. It was a family grief, and I did not want to intrude on it.

The small crowd of people had dispersed, and Cronlin stood scowling at the door of that other compartment. I wondered what they were going to do, with one murder in South Australia and the other in Western Australia—and possibly Cronlin was wondering too.

Clive came out of the compartment just then and saw me. He had a few low-voiced words with Cronlin and then approached me.

"Shall we go along and get some tea? They're serving it early."

I nodded, remembered the wretched telegram, and blushed furiously. As I walked down the corridor ahead of him I tried to shake my hair forward so that it would hide my glowing face.

The lounge car was crowded, and people were talking with their heads close together and almost in whispers. The talk stopped with embarrassing suddenness as Clive and I walked in, and heads turned from all parts of the car to stare at us. I saw Mary with two other women, and Eileen hanging over her chair, looking puzzled and excited. Mary tried to catch my eye, but I would not look at her, and Clive took my arm and steered me over toward the piano. He drew up a chair for me and seated himself on the piano stool.

"We can have a little privacy here," he said in a low voice. "There are some things that we ought to talk over."

"Yes," I agreed simply. "He was murdered, wasn't he?"

Clive nodded, while a worried line appeared between his brows. "With a razor, probably—the same as the girl. This wasn't such a good job, though—his collar was in the way. He'd had a bang on the head, too."

"Oh God!" I moaned softly. "I'm glad we're getting off this train in a couple of hours—I've never been so glad about anything in my life. I couldn't stand much more of it. I won't go on to Perth, either—I'll stay in Kalgoorlie. I suppose they'll hold me there anyway. And I'll have to tell the police what Jimmy said—about Cleo, I mean."

Clive said, "Yes. That's what I wanted to talk to you about. We must tell them, and the sooner the better."

The tea was brought in then, and we were silent for a while. I noticed presently that Eileen had edged over and was eating her cake right beside us.

"I suppose you won't have any trouble getting on to Perth, will you?" I asked Clive, with Eileen's flapping ears in mind.

He shrugged. "I'll be held up for a while, almost undoubtedly— there's the medical evidence. I may even be hauled back to South Australia on that score."

I nodded absently, with my eyes on Eileen, who was pretending an absorbed interest in the scenery.

"I'd like to take you to dinner when we get to Kalgoorlie," Clive said suddenly. "It ought to be safe enough, after that warning from the practical and farsighted Marge."

My face started to burn again, and after two false starts I said feebly, "You watch your step. Even Marge would have to agree that Sale's richest son is not to be sneezed at."

Brewster appeared at the door and, after a competent glance

around, made straight for the piano.

He stood looking down at us for a moment and then asked amiably, "Miss Peters, does that little box of paints in your suitcase mean that you are a painter?"

Chapter Twenty-Five
THE TOGGLE BOLT

A PAINTBOX! So I was to be accused of sneaking around and finishing Uncle Joe's masterpieces—and that would fit Cronlin's theory very nicely. I was trying to make it appear that Uncle Joe was unbalanced and should be put under restraint, so that I could get control of Cleo's part of his money, because I was impersonating Cleo.

I set my jaw and said sharply, "No. I don't paint and I don't own a paintbox. If there is one in my luggage, then someone else put it there."

The detective sat down and wrinkled his brow thoughtfully. "The suitcase *had* been disturbed," he admitted, "as though someone had been turning things up."

"Do you mean my own suitcase or the one I'm using?" I asked.

"Your own. But if you've lost your memory how do you know that you don't paint?"

"My memory has been coming back—I have nearly all of it now."

"Temporary amnesia," Clive murmured.

"I have never painted nor even bought a paintbox," I added emphatically. I hoped it was the truth, too. My sojourn in Sydney, just before taking the transcontinental trip, was still vague. I remembered Cleo and Marge and some other friends there, but it was not at all clear.

Clive raised his eyebrows at me and indicated Brewster with a movement of his head. "Better him about Jimmy, I mean."

I nodded and plunged into my story. I kept my voice as low as I could, but I wished uneasily that we could have more privacy for the recital. Eileen bothered me, too, for she kept edging closer, until at last Brewster caught sight of her. He said sharply, "Run away, little girl—this is not for your ears," and Eileen flounced off, looking offended. She went over to one of the windows and flattened the tip of her nose against it.

When I had finished Brewster said, "Hmm," and then, after thinking it over for a bit, he said, "Hmm," again. After which he observed, "Singular!" and studied the floor for a while.

I waited in silence, and he presently raised his head and looked at me. "I don't understand why you didn't tell us this before."

I had expected that, and I said unhappily, "I should have, of course— but I didn't want to get Jimmy into trouble, and I disliked casting such a slur on Cleo. After all, it might not have been true."

Brewster shook his head, wrinkled up his forehead, and said, "Singular!" again. He stared, unseeing, down the length of the car—and a timid-looking man, seated in the line of his eye, went pale and started to squirm.

"There's one thing I've remembered that perhaps I ought to tell you," I said after a moment. "There's an extra pocket at the bottom of my suitcase, where I keep my passport and other papers. It isn't very noticeable, and I expect the people at Albury missed it and simply identified us on that application blank and the snapshot of me."

Brewster knew all about the pocket, for he merely nodded and said, "Something like that. Anyway, the hospital says this Cleo accepted the name of Virginia Peters without protest or explanation—so that whatever was going on she was in it too."

"You don't mean 'too,' " I said sharply. "I was in on nothing. I've told you the truth—that I lost my memory—and Doctor Butler will bear me out."

"Doctor Butler can't be sure," Brewster pointed out. "He believes you lost your memory, but there is no way for him, or you either, to prove it. Now, have you any theory as to why Cleo Ballister did not correct the people at the hospital and give her right name?"

"Yes," I said at once. "She probably thought it was a scream, from what I can remember of her."

"A scream?"

"A joke. A—well—funny."

"I see," said Brewster. "And when she caught up with you, why didn't she tell you about it?"

"She saw that I did not recognize her, I suppose—and perhaps she heard me talking to Clive about my lost memory—I don't know. But in any case she apparently made up her mind to take my identity. It's understandable, because she was in a tight spot, with Jimmy threatening her. If she didn't herself have a hand in the death of the man who fell downstairs, I think she must have known who did. I suppose she thought she wouldn't be recognized after the disguise of the veil and the red hair—but somebody did recognize her—and she was killed because she was recognized and because she knew something."

"Thanks very much," said Brewster, with just a touch of sarcasm. "And now let's hear why the other was killed—this Jimmy."

"He knew too. He realized it as soon as I convinced him that I was not Cleo."

"Simple as that," said Brewster. "Go on."

"I can't. I mean I've told you all I know—and that's what you'd call dinkum."

He almost cracked a smile, but changed his mind at the last minute. Instead he stood up, thanked me formally, and made off.

I glanced around at the crowded car and saw that we had had an absorbed audience. They could not have heard what we said, but apparently the gestures had been fascinating. I turned back to Clive and found him grinning at me.

"Quite a trio—you, Marge, and Cleo."

I blushed once more and took a hasty sip of cold tea. "All right, so we were quite a trio. Met regularly to compare notes on how much money we'd been able to dig out of our fellow men."

"I think you were the odd man out," he said, still laughing at me. "You don't look like Cleo, and I don't suppose you look like Marge, either."

I shook my head. "Marge is a blonde too, out of a bottle recommended by Cleo. But if I look more refined than the other two, that only makes me more dangerous. Because what was I flocking with them for if I'm not a bird of their feather?"

"You make it a little confusing," he said, "but I think I understand. However, a fool there was, and so I still want to take you out to dinner tonight."

"I'll come," I agreed, "if I'm not behind bars."

I shivered, quite involuntarily, and looked up to find Eileen staring at me with her mouth hanging open.

"Now, don't you pay any attention, honey," I said quickly. "I was only trying to be funny."

"But"—her eyes slid around, and she came closer to me—"what are all the policemen going to do?" she whispered. "Mother won't tell me anything, but I know there's a madman on the train who's going around killing people, and I know he killed poor Uncle Jimmy and that lady with the yellow hair. Tell me about it, Auntie, please."

"I don't know a thing that I could tell you about, sugar."

"Sugar," Clive repeated, and sounded intrigued. "Do you suppose you'll ever call me sugar?"

At the same time Mary called sharply, "Eileen! Come here!"

Eileen went off reluctantly, and I knew from the sound of Mary's voice that she had me in the doghouse. She had wanted us to join her when we first came in and was now miffed to the point of giving us the aloof treatment.

I stood up and looked out of the window, trying to be casual but feeling self-conscious. I knew that they were all looking at me from behind their fans, so to speak, and I had lost my aplomb. For a while I didn't see anything, and then the landscape forced itself on my attention. Trees—plenty of them— whirling past the window. I stood there, absorbed, until Clive gave me a pat on the shoulder.

"Your petticoat is showing," he whispered, "and everybody is looking at you."

"What's a petticoat?" I whispered back. "I don't wear things like that."

"Yes, you do. I just saw it."

I straightened up and turned around, raising my chin a little against the silent appraisal before me, and then I fled. As I made my way to my own car I wondered how I could ever have believed that acting was my profession.

One of Brewster's fellow detectives was standing in the corridor, and he asked alertly, "Where are you going, miss?

"I want to see if I can be of any help to Mrs. Ballister."

"No, miss, if you please. They are being questioned, and the sergeant detective doesn't want to be disturbed."

I looked along the corridor and saw the uniformed Western Australia policeman standing directly outside the door of my compartment with folded arms. Cronlin was nowhere in sight.

"Hadn't you better go back to the lounge?" the hovering detective suggested.

"No," I said crossly. "I have a headache and my petticoat shows. I want to lie down. I'll go into Uncle Joe's compartment."

He looked at me as though he thought I belonged in an asylum, but he walked along and opened Uncle Joe's door for me. The compartment was empty, and I went in and stretched out on the seat.

My feet were aching and throbbing, and I realized that I still wore the red shoes. There must have been a pair of my own shoes in that suitcase, I thought fretfully; why hadn't I looked for them when I'd had the chance? They'd *have* to give me that suitcase before we got into Kalgoorlie. I looked at my watch—4:15; we were due in about an hour.

I closed my eyes and tried to think of Sydney and of Cleo, but for some reason Marge kept getting in the way. Marge had a good position as a secretary, but she was saving up to go to Hollywood and crash the movies. She had attached herself to Cleo with a vim, and Cleo didn't mind because Marge helped her out financially whenever it was necessary.

Things were coming back to me now—rapidly.

Cleo had had an arrangement at a nightclub in Sydney, and that was when she made the application for a driver's license. She had intended to buy a car on time, and then her engagement had ceased, so she kept the application in her purse until she could again consider buying the car. Her passport was probably in Marge's bookcase—she had often bunked in with Marge when her funds were low. When I had met her in July she had been preparing to go away—and then she had gone and come back again and, with all her garrulity, would not say where she had been. Marge was sure she had been off with a "boy"— they were all "boys" to Marge. Her own boys were not numerous, which puzzled and distressed her, but she always said, "Just you wait until I'm a star, and then I'll have all the boys after me."

But Marge wasn't getting me anywhere, and I tried to turn my mind back to Cleo, only she was elusive, somehow.

I opened my eyes, and they fell on Uncle Joe's latest painting. He had balanced it on a suitcase, leaning against the wall, and its back was to me. Was it still the way he had left it, I wondered, or had someone tampered with it? Curiosity pulled me off the seat, and I went over and picked the thing up. At first I thought it was the same, and then I saw that there was a slight difference. Some object had been painted into the extended hand of the aborigine—something that looked like a stick, with a pair of wings near the top.

I stared for a while in growing bewilderment, until quite suddenly I realized what it was. Jimmy's last, painful words. The painted object was supposed to be a toggle bolt.

Chapter Twenty-Six
THE MISSING HAND

I PUT THE BLOCK BACK in its place and sat down again. A toggle bolt—there was something familiar about that. Where had I heard of it, anyway? Old John—he had sent me out to buy one. He had wanted to hang a picture, a particularly heavy one of a kangaroo, I remembered, and he had said a toggle bolt was what he needed, so I had gone out and bought it. That was how I had been able to recognize it in the painting. But why was it painted in there, and what was the connection with Jimmy's last, gasping words?

I shuddered, and then Uncle Joe's lizard barked, and I sprang to my feet in horror. I discovered that the thing was in a small box studded with air holes, but I still felt that it was uncomfortably close to me, and I left the compartment with more speed than dignity.

Cronlin and Brewster were in the corridor, talking rather heatedly, and Uncle Joe's voice boomed from the interior of the compartment.

"I'm blowed if I think you have the right—but we'll stay over one day, anyway. We'll bury poor Jimmy. He's always liked Kalgoorlie—it's where his cobbers are."

He appeared at the door, puffing and blowing, and Brewster said pacifically, "All right, Mr. Ballister—no offense. It's just that we want you to stand by for a day or so."

"One day!" Uncle Joe corrected him fiercely. He pushed past them and pounded along to his own compartment, with Wilfred creeping in his wake.

I slipped into any compartment and found Aunt Esther sitting up with her hat on and looking much more composed. All her things were packed, and her gloves and bag lay in her lap.

"You're all ready to get off," I smiled, sitting beside her.

"Oh dear," she said faintly, and began to twist the gloves through her fingers. "I don't know what's to become of us—it's dreadful."

133

"You mustn't worry about it," I said inadequately.

"But I can't understand it. Joe keeps saying it's nothing to do with us—but it is—it must be! That girl was our niece—and now Jimmy— Of course it has to do with us—I don't think the other passengers are involved at all. And then that girl—Cleo. You know, it seems she was the red-haired woman who stayed with us in Perth. Why would she do that?"

I shook my head. I didn't know, exactly—I could only guess. I didn't think Cleo would go with the express intention of tripping her uncle down the stairs, but she had disguised herself—and why had she done that? Someone must have told her to come—and paid her way—because she'd had no money at that time.

"They're even saying that poor George was murdered too," Aunt Esther said distractedly. "They think there was a string tied across the top of the stairs, and he tripped over it when he started down. I told them it was nonsense— there's nothing to tie a string to on one side— only a blank wall." Her tears spilled over, and she sobbed, "It must be one of us. Money is a curse—it's the money."

"Please," I said uncomfortably, "you mustn't get all upset again. Look, I'll have to pack—maybe you could help me. I'll see if they'll give me my own clothes."

I went into the corridor, where Brewster, now aided by the other detective and the West Australia trooper, was still arguing with Cronlin. I could not hear what they were saying, although I tried, and when Brewster caught sight of me he stopped in mid-sentence. He nodded to me and then politely requested me to check in at a hotel in Kalgoorlie.

"You understand that we'd like to have you where we can question you when it's necessary."

I understood and said so, feeling vastly relieved. They were not arresting me—at least not immediately.

"Stay at the same hotel as the Ballisters, if you please, miss," Brewster added.

"Yes, certainly," I agreed. "But could you let me have some of my clothes? These shoes are killing me. And I need a hat and a purse."

This started a wrangle, during which it emerged that they felt they should hold my things but that it was just as necessary to hold Cleo's. The West Australia cop passed the remark that the poor girl—myself— wouldn't be allowed naked in Kalgoorlie, and was told by Brewster that when he wanted any funny business he'd ask for it.

In the end they gave me a pair of brown shoes, a brown purse, and a hat of natural-colored straw. I was also allowed a brown paper parcel containing my toothbrush and other necessities. The toothbrush reminded me that I had been using Cleo's, and after wrinkling my nose over the thought I offered to hand hers back to them. The West Australia cop, still benevolent as he had been about my clothes, told me to keep it.

"Tyke it, miss—if you don't want it on your teeth, you can use it for something else." He lowered his voice and added, "Don't get them narked, or they may take back the clothes, and then you'll be naked again."

The idea sent him off into a gale of silent laughter, and I thanked him and backed away, blushing. But I felt immensely cheered. At least I was still free.

The train stopped, and I began to make for the end of the corridor, but Cronlin called, "Hold on there, miss—this is only Parkeston. We'll be at Kalgoorlie in ten minutes."

I blushed again and slipped into my own compartment, hoping they didn't think that I had been trying to make a getaway.

Aunt Esther was on her way out with as many of her bags and bundles as she could carry. I said, "Why don't you leave them here, and we'll keep the door open? We can't miss Kalgoorlie—I hear it's the end of the line."

"Yes—yes, I suppose so," she said abstractedly, and sat down again. I began to clean up a little, and she watched me, fanning herself with her handkerchief. It had become much hotter, and I realized that the air conditioning had been turned off.

Wilfred burst in, flushed and excited, and asked, "Are you all packed, Mother? Are you ready?"

"Yes, yes, I'm all right," she told him. "What about Joe? He's the one we have to bother about."

"I'm getting him done—I'm seeing to it," he said, flying off again.

Aunt Esther sighed. "Wilfred was always a good boy—he's been a blessing to me."

I murmured something which was immediately lost in a series of roars coming from Uncle Joe's compartment. Aunt Esther and I rose as one person and hurried down the corridor to the scene of the storm.

Uncle Joe was tearing his latest painting to pieces—literally, with the penknife that was attached to one end of his heavy gold watch chain. Wilfred had flattened himself against the window and was saying feebly, "Please, please—"

A lot of Uncle Joe's words were blurred, but I caught a part of what he was saying.

"—bloody barsted—my best work—the best thing I ever did. If I ever get my 'ands on 'im—"

Aunt Esther said, "Joe!" and he stopped and looked at her. "Do you want to land us all in jail?" she asked furiously. "Upon my word, you ought to be ashamed of yourself—carrying on like a child."

Uncle Joe dropped what remained of the picture and sank down onto the seat. "I took a lot of trouble over that one—I was going to finish it in Perth—quietly at home." He thought for a moment, and fury mounted in him once more. "It was my bloody masterpiece, Es— don't you understand that? And some bloody barsted has ruined it."

"Hush," said Aunt Esther. "Are you packed? You know very well that you can remember the thing and paint it again as soon as we get home."

Mary and Eileen came up behind us, and Eileen observed that I looked very nice. I told her that she looked nice too, but the kid pouted. "I'd be all right if Mother would let me take the flower garden off my hat."

I mentally agreed wholeheartedly but held my peace, and Mary, her face an angry red, told Eileen that the wreath on her hat was the height of fashion and she was to leave it there.

"She's such a trouble," she told me. "Opinionated about her clothes—and she even tells me what I should wear—me. And she's only a little girl."

Mary looked as though a little telling from someone would do no harm, but I clucked disapprovingly and tried to look sympathetic.

Uncle Joe, after puffing and blowing through his walrus for a while, began to cheer up. "Well—'ere we are in Kalgoorlie. Ahr, there's a town for you. Spent my youth 'ere. Jimmy loved it too, poor lad. But I 'ad it earlier. The golden mile—in those days—"

"We'd better finish your packing, Uncle Joe," Wilfred suggested timidly.

"No 'urry, boy—keep your blasted shirt on. To think of all the time I spent in Kalgoorlie—and one day I was rich, and the next poor—ahr, those were the days. Nothing like a young mining town for a gay time."

Mary and Eileen departed, and Aunt Esther began to fasten Uncle Joe's bag.

"No, no, Mother—wait," Wilfred fussed. "These things have to go in."

Uncle Joe ignored them and turned his eyes on me. I could see that nothing was going to stop him from telling about his youth and Kalgoorlie.

"It's not the same today—it's a city now—center of one of the most famous gold fields in the world. And me right on the spot here when it grew up, and I never really struck it rich. But poor old George came down for a week and got in on something. Just shows you—you never know your luck."

The speed of the train had slowed a little, and through the window I caught glimpses of population—people and houses. I was glad that we were nearly in, and I felt better than I had for quite some time. I knew who I was—I had my memory and my own clothes, and I had done nothing really wrong—I knew that. But I was in a tight spot, and I'd need to fight.

I glanced down at the ragged pieces of Uncle Joe's late masterpiece and thought of the toggle bolt in the hand of the aborigine. I'd gather up those pieces, I decided, and paste them together later.

" 'Ere we are—'urry up now—we're getting in," Uncle Joe shouted as hle train began to slow. I was carried out into the corridor by the sheer weight of them, but I managed at last to make my way back into the compartment. I hastily gathered up the pieces of the picture and studied each one carefully—but the painted hand holding the toggle bolt was missing entirely.

Chapter Twenty-Seven
FAMILY CARPENTER

I LOOKED FOR THAT MISSING SCRAP very carefully, but I did not find it. The train had come into the Kalgoorlie station and stopped, and people were getting off, but I lingered behind and searched the poor of the corridor.

I had to give up at last. I was sure, by that time, that the scrap meant something to someone and had been disposed of. It must mean something, I thought, since Jimmy had muttered "toggle bolt" with almost his last breath. And what had he meant, I wondered, by "The carpenter"? A carpenter would probably use toggle bolts, but I couldn't make any more sense out of it than that. No one knew about those last words of Jimmy's but myself, and I felt that I must keep quiet about them for my own protection. I had not told even Clive.

Kalgoorlie was a city, with a railway station to match—no corrugated-iron-roofed shacks here. Uncle Joe was loud in proclaiming that he knew it well and had known it when—until the sight of the connecting train to Perth put him into a bit of a temper. He got hold of Cronlin and complained hotly about not being able to take it.

"We'd be in Perth tomorrow morning—and a man and his family like to spend Christmas at home."

Wilfred showed a little burst of spirit at this point and said, "Uncle Joe, there is no help for this situation, and we might as well accept it. Let's get to the hotel and make the best of it—and do all we can to help the investigation along. After all, they were our relatives—and Mother was fond of Jimmy."

Uncle Joe looked a bit deflated, puffed through his walrus once or twice, and then said quite mildly, "All right, boy—no need to bring out the 'ymnbooks. Good job we are staying—p'r'aps we *can* 'elp them along a bit."

Clive came up and said to me, "I'll be along later to fetch you for dinner. I'm tooling off with the constabulary now. Where are you staying?"

"I don't know," I said a bit forlornly. "But I expect the constabulary will be able to tell you."

He nodded. "Right. I'll find you. About seven, then."

He went off, and I felt unreasonably neglected and deserted. These people were not related to me. I had no claim on them, and perhaps they didn't like having me in their midst. After all, I had brought them nothing but misfortune—or it seemed that way. I was wondering whether to suggest that I go off by myself, when I was handed a telegram.

Will arrive Kalgoorlie first possible train. John Osborne.

I read it over three times, and felt as though I had been anchored after an indefinite drifting. I'd have someone who knew me to back me up—someone who was making all haste to come and help me. I felt almost happy, and so utterly relieved that I began to cry.

I was immediately ashamed of this display of emotion, the more so when I saw that Eileen had noticed me and had run to Aunt Esther, who came over to me at once and offered sympathy. She was very kind and said, "Don't worry about it, my dear—we're all in the same boat. Suppose we leave Joe and Wilfred to take care of the luggage and we'll go on ahead to the hotel. I want them to see about our things in the baggage coach too. There's no use sending them on to Perth yet, as we don't know how long we'll be held up here."

"I'm all right," I said uncomfortably. "Just letting off steam. But I think it's a good idea to go on to the hotel—you look worn out yourself."

We got away, after a bit of a rumpus with Uncle Joe, who wanted to stay at his pet hotel. However, Aunt Esther knew it, too, and flatly refused to go there.

When we arrived at the hotel of Aunt Esther's choice she invited me to share a room with her.

"It's more companionable, don't you think?" she suggested. "At home I like my own room, but when I travel it seems nicer to have someone with me."

I agreed, with a grateful feeling that she was considering my feelings more than her own.

We were given a corner room—big and comfortable and not too hot. Aunt Esther went through her usual routine of unpacking her necessities and disposing them tidily, and she observed, as she moved about, that when Joe turned up with the rest of the luggage she'd be able to get out a change of shoes.

"Don't tantalize me," I said, opening my brown paper parcel. "Now, shall I unpack this vast amount of my possessions or leave them in their wrapping paper and pick them out as I need them?"

Aunt Esther said, "Tch, tch, tch, tch."

"Oh, it's all right," I assured her cheerfully. "As long as I have one costume that belongs to me, I feel satisfied."

Uncle Joe presently burst in, followed by a hotel attendant with Aunt Esther's other suitcase. She began to deal competently with them, while Uncle Joe flung himself into a chair and mopped his perspiring forehead. His walrus was straggling untidily, and his tie was twisted around under one ear.

"We were mobbed, Es," he said excitedly. "Reporters. Train was early, so you missed them. They had me talking, there, I can tell you."

Aunt Esther raised a startled face from one of the suitcases and looked at him. "Joe! Heavens above and the earth beneath! What did you say? You know it will be in all the Perth papers. Oh, I do hope you were careful. What *did* you say?"

"Don't worry your head about it," said Uncle Joe, still mopping. "I know those blokes, and I know how to handle them. They followed us here, y'know—they're downstairs now—Wilfred's with 'em. Can't get away—they won't let him go. He's a bit of an ass in some ways, that boy—just like his father. Now I merely said, 'See you later, chaps,' and walked off."

Aunt Esther frowned and folded her lips at the reference to Wilfred, and then said, as though speaking to herself, "I'd better unpack a few things—no way of knowing how long we'll be detained here."

"Don't you unpack a ruddy thing," Uncle Joe boomed. "We're leaving tomorrow—I'll pull strings. I'm not going to spend me Christmas here."

"My." But Aunt Esther made the correction absentmindedly, and Uncle Joe banged out of the room without taking any notice of it. She unpacked some of her things, despite his assurance of a speedy departure, and hung them away in the closet.

I helped her as much as I could, and then had a bath and donned the fresh underwear that I had been allowed to roll into my paper parcel. Clive was announced before I was half dressed, but I finished with due care, and when at last I went downstairs I felt clean and smart.

I had barely stepped out of the elevator when Clive grabbed me, rushed me out a side door, and threw me into a cab. It started immediately, and I was thrown back against the seat.

"Kidnapping?" I asked, catching my breath.

"Reporters."

"What's the news? I mean the inside dope. Am I still on the spot?"

He laughed softly, took my hand, and said, "When I go courting I prefer not to discuss the seamy side of life."

"You don't say!" I murmured. "Are you courting this evening?"

"I think I must be. I shaved twice—and no other emergency ever induces me to shave twice."

"Then you've been courting before. No luck apparently, either."

"You don't know enough of the circumstances to judge properly," he said with dignity. "A gentleman may go courting many times before he throws his hat into the ring."

"You mean this is just a trial performance? If I don't stack up, I'll lose you, and also the chance of giving Sale the raspberry?"

His hand tightened on my wrist and twisted it slightly. "You cast one more slur at Sale—only one—and I'll take you back and throw you to the reporters."

"I beg pardon, I'm sure," I said feebly. "Let's go and eat—and all honor and glory to Sale. I'm getting to be just like you people—I want me cup of tea and whatever goes with it every two hours."

We drew up at a small hotel on a side street, where Clive said he'd heard the food was good and where the reporters probably would not find us.

As soon as we were comfortably seated in the restaurant Clive went on with his courting. He picked up a strand of my hair and wound it around his finger. "I'm very fond of natural curls," he said, pulling gently. "I can't stand these artificial-looking perms that most of the girls get."

"Well," I said mildly, "I hate to disillusion people—and especially I hate to disillusion one of Sale's finest—because you probably picked me out, thinking that I'd be fairly inexpensive with no permanent-wave costs—but my ringlets were disciplined at one of the finest hairdressing salons—at double the price of the ordinary perm."

He dropped my expensive curl and said, "Cheat. At least the ordinary perm is obviously a perm. It's false pretenses."

"So is your second shave," I replied equably. "You want me to think you have a skin like a baby—whereas, at this time of day, your face is usually of the ordinary nutmeg-grater variety." I glanced around idly and then added with sudden consternation, "Oh, Lord help us!"

Uncle Joe was making his way among the tables, followed by Mary and Wilfred. He saw us a moment after I had seen him and came bounding over with his face beaming.

"Well, well, well, fancy your two finding this place! This is the 'otel where I always come when I'm on me own. I'd be staying 'ere now, but Es thinks it's not befitting."

He laughed heartily, summoned waiters with a wave of his arm, and had another table wedged up against ours. When the three of them were seated with us I felt as though we were back on the train—and the pleasure I'd had in forgetting about it was gone.

Uncle Joe immediately launched into a lusty history of himself, Kalgoorlie, and the golden mile. Mary, who was sitting next to me, listened respectfully for a while and then turned to me and began to talk quietly.

"Uncle Joe says we're not to talk about the dreadful things on the train, so I suppose we really shouldn't—but I can't get it out of my head."

I nodded rather dispiritedly, and she put her elbows on her table—which moved it slightly away from ours and left a crack down the middle.

"Oh, look at the dashed thing," she said, trying to move it back. "I suppose one leg is shorter than the others, or something. Eileen should be here—she'd mend it in a jiff. You wouldn't think it of her, would you? She's such a lady, and so careful of her manners—but she's a regular little carpenter."

Chapter Twenty-Eight
A BEASTLY STORY

THERE MUST HAVE BEEN some reflection in my face of my rather startled reaction to Mary's remark, for she asked, "What's the matter?"

"Nothing—swallowed a piece of hot potato. That's odd about Eileen, isn't it? Carpentry, of all things."

"Yes—she knows all about the various tools and what to do with them. You couldn't stump her on anything in that line."

"It's interesting," I said thoughtfully "You never know what children are going to take to."

Mary agreed that you didn't and started a long tale about an aunt of hers who was the belle of the town and yet liked nothing better than to spend her time under an automobile with a wrench in her hand.

I listened for a while and then took refuge in my own puzzled thoughts. Eileen would know what a toggle bolt was, I reflected—in fact, she'd know a lot. I'd have to talk to her. She'd know, for instance, who, in the family, was the adult carpenter. Mary probably knew that herself, though. But she was still working her way through the story about her aunt, and when that was finished the talk became general, so that even Uncle Joe's reminiscences had to be shelved.

We were working on coffee and liqueurs by this time, and I had to warn myself not to become indiscreet and mention the carpenter and the toggle bolt. I remembered Old John hanging his heavy picture and explaining that the toggle bolt was driven through the wall and that the two little wings on the end then opened out and so made the bolt secure enough to bear a considerable weight. I thought about it and decided that if you wanted to tie a piece of string across the stairs you could use a toggle bolt for the wall side—except that you wouldn't need to, really—probably even a thumbtack would do.

Clive reached for our check at this point and said, "Awfully sorry we have to leave—it's been very pleasant—but I promised my friends we'd show up. Come on, Virgineeah."

"You'd better call me Ginny," I said, getting to my feet. "You can't play around with it so much."

Uncle Joe said he was sorry that we had to go, and appeared to mean it. He said it was a "shime" three times—and three times Wilfred winced but forebore to correct him. In the end he waved us a cheery good-by and told us to "be'ave"—and Wilfred winced for the fourth time.

When we had left them and were out on the street I asked, "What friends?"

Clive took my arm companionably and admitted, "I can't recall their names offhand—but I prefer to do my courting when Uncle Joe isn't around. He puts me off."

"Never mind about Uncle Joe," I said. "Maybe you could find your friends' names by running through the telephone book."

"The next time I have a week or two to spare I'll do that," he said, pasting it thickly with sarcasm. "Don't you know that this is a metropolis? What makes you behave as though every Australian city had a population of about fifty?"

"I'm a dizzy American," I said meekly. "Kindly excuse it."

The weather was nice—still warm, but no longer uncomfortable, now that the blazing sun had gone. We walked slowly along the street, and someone with squeaky shoes strolled behind us.

"He ought to have them oiled," Clive observed idly. "It draws attention to him—and tails should never be heard, although they must, occasionally, be seen."

"Tails!" I gasped. "Do you mean they're—he's following us?"

"Of course," he said reasonably. "Somebody has to sit down at the station house and do the brainwork—and in the meantime they don't want us all to run away."

"It's no use," I groaned. "The evening's spoiled. We can't have any peace while this thing is hanging over us. I might as well go back to the hotel."

"To mope? What good will that do?"

"I'm not going to mope," I said crossly. "I want to have a talk with Eileen."

"Eileen?" he asked, astounded. "What does she have that I haven't?"

"Nothing. I mean—I just thought she might know something."

I wondered whether, after all, I ought to tell Clive about Jimmy's strange words, but as I hesitated he spoke again.

"You can't go and talk to the kid now—they shove her into bed early, and they'd be a bit sticky about it if you went in and shook her awake for a social chat. If you must talk about the thing, we'll go somewhere for a drink, and I'll listen."

I pictured myself waking Eileen out of a sound sleep to ask her who in the family had taught her carpentry, and said, "All right—where's the pub?"

"I believe there's a place up the street here," he said, "and don't try to speak Australian until you've learned it. Ladies don't go to pubs."

"Yes, they do. They merely call it a shovel instead of a spade. Is this place you're looking for fit for our tail? He looks like a family man."

"If it's fit for a future matron of Sale," said Clive sternly, "it's fit for a bobby. Especially for one whose shoes squeak.'

We went into a cocktail lounge of sorts and found a small table to ourselves. After we had ordered I settled back with a sigh and said, "I wish we had something more pleasant to talk about than this wretched business."

He grinned at me. "We have—but I can't get you to stay on the subject. I'm beginning to wonder if you're going to regale my evening homecoming to our little home in Sale with tales of how bad the children have been and what are we going to do about it—and when are we going to be able to afford a new carpet for the drawing-room."

"We can get along without a drawing-room," I said carelessly. "The only drawing I do is doodling on the phone book when I'm giving the grocery order. And as for the children, I can do a lot better than that when I want to crab—like 'Where were you last night, you drunken bum?'"

He did a Wilfred wince, and I realized that I shouldn't have used the last expression.

"Oh well," I said by way of apology, "you've been to the movies and read American books."

"Yes," he conceded, "but I don't think Sale would accept that word. Of course we have the cinema there."

"Good old Sale."

" 'Snothing, my dear girl. There is also a radio station in Sale. I helped Mr. Gilchrist once. Read an announcement for him."

"The next announcement will be read by Dr. Butler and in no way reflects the usual standard of our announcements."

"I think you're getting sleepy," said Clive. "He sold the station."
"What!"

"Mr. Gilchrist sold his radio station."

"Oh," I said, "I thought you meant he'd sold the railway station. I was wondering if you'd bought it, and I was going to try and sell you the Brooklyn Bridge. I suppose Mr. Gilchrist has a couple of daughters?"

"How'd you know?" he asked suspiciously.

"Guessed. Pretty girls?"

"Yes. Smart, too. One was in medical school with me—got higher marks than I did."

"She probably brought the teacher an apple."

"No," he said regretfully. "Smart—as I said. The other one let me come to her wedding."

"Ah well," I sighed, fishing for the cherry in my drink, "think how their eyes will bug out when you return in triumph with a beautiful American on your arm."

"Well, I'm glad to know that you understand the situation," he said, sitting up "Now—"

But we were interrupted. A man, who turned out to be an old friend of Clive's, joined us, and after he had been introduced to me they fell into rapid talk of past, present, and future. I listened for a while and then found myself drifting back into the dark thoughts that lay in my mind.

That paintbox that they had found in my suitcase—why was it there? Planted, of course—but by whom? Jimmy? He had been scared, and perhaps he had been finishing Uncle Joe's paintings, with some idea of getting the old boy put away in an asylum. And then he could marry Cleo, and she'd get her half of the money right away. Only, would she? It was doubtful. More probably the money would simply be tied up. Tied up! Aunt Esther wanted the money tied up—she'd like nothing better. She hated the way Uncle Joe was throwing it around—Wilfred's money. And now that Cleo was dead, Wilfred would probably get it all.

Clive's friend was saying good-by and presently took himself off. I finished my drink and refused another. "I don't know what time it is, but I expect that fellow with the loud shoes ought to be getting home to his wife and seven."

"You Americans are born restless," said Clive. "I don't know how you stand going to bed at night and just lying there until morning."

It was about eleven o'clock when we got back to the hotel, and Clive took me in the side door. "You never know about reporters," he explained. "They may have no interest in you at all—but on the other hand—"

"Good night," I said. "I've enjoyed it. In fact, it was bonzer."

"I could smack you," he said unexpectedly, "right across your charming mouth without half trying." He pushed me into what he called the lift, and I went on up alone.

I crept into our corner room quietly, in case Aunt Esther was asleep, and switched on the small bedside lamp—and then I stood and gaped.

Eileen was asleep in my bed.

Aunt Esther raised her head from her pillow and blinked at me. "Oh, it's you, my dear. Eileen came in to talk—she was lonely—and we both fell asleep." I nodded, and Aunt Esther stretched and turned to the other bed. "Eileen! Wake up, child—you'll have to go back to your own room."

Eileen woke up readily enough, but she was reluctant to leave us. She said she was afraid, all alone in that room by herself, and at last I offered to go with her and stay until she went to sleep or her mother got back.

I helped her into bed and smoothed the covers over her, and she lay quietly looking at the ceiling. I sat in an armchair and was drawn back into my speculations about Aunt Esther.

I simply could not believe that she had killed Cleo or Jimmy—and it didn't make sense, either, because in that case she wouldn't bother to get Uncle Joe's money tied up—she would kill him too. And that seemed to be true of Mary and Wilfred as well.

Then who had planted the paintbox in my suitcase? Jimmy hadn't finished Uncle Joe's paintings, because what was the use, to Jimmy, of getting Uncle Joe's money tied up? Jimmy wanted to spend money. But Aunt Esther didn't—she'd rather see it saved—for Wilfred and Eileen. Perhaps Jimmy had planted the paintbox in my suitcase for Aunt Esther's sake—perhaps he knew what she was doing—and the danger in it. And perhaps he had been caught and killed while he was in that compartment.

Cleo had said she could get money out of her relatives. Blackmail, probably. She had not killed Uncle George, but she had seen the person who did, and she had come out of her room and removed that string across the staircase—an impulsive cover-up, and just like Cleo. The murderer had seen her do it, and so had Jimmy, and she was in trouble—so she had run back to Sydney. She had thought it over for a while and then decided to go back again and try blackmail.

Eileen turned her head on the pillow and looked at me. "You know, Auntie, Uncle Jimmy told me a beastly story, once, about a man who lived here in Kalgoorlie. Uncle Jimmy and Uncle Joe had dinner with this man, and then the next morning they found him with his head almost cut off with a razor. And two other men thought Uncle Joe did it."

Chapter Twenty-Nine
THE WAY TO DO A MURDER

UNCLE JOE. Of course, I thought wildly, of course it was Uncle Joe—and Jimmy had realized it when we were standing at that station out on the desert.

I looked at Eileen and said cautiously, "Everyone calls Uncle Joe 'the carpenter,' I suppose?"

"Oh yes," she said, "but I'm good at it too. He taught me."

"I know," I whispered, and found myself staring at the door while drops of perspiration started out on my forehead. There had been some sort of sound—and in a moment it was repeated. The knob turned, and Uncle Joe walked in. He was alone, and I knew instantly that he had been listening outside—and that he almost certainly had heard what Eileen had told me. He said, " 'Ullo," and closed the door after him, and the room was dark again.

I stumbled to my feet, and my voice came out high and thin. "Wait a minute—I'll turn on the light."

"No," said Uncle Joe, "we don't need a light."

But I made my way to the bed and fumbled with sweating hands until I found the bedside lamp and switched it on.

Uncle Joe was sitting on a straight chair, his hands kneading themselves in a continuous, restless motion and his eyes on Eileen's bed. I stood with my hand frozen on the lamp, literally unable to move, and all the time I kept thinking monotonously, *Eileen is his favorite—he loves her—she's his favorite.*

The silence finally bore down on me with such terrific pressure that I had to speak into it. "Where are Mary and Wilfred?" I asked, and marveled that the thin, sick voice could be mine.

Uncle Joe started and turned to look at me. "They're out kicking up their 'eels—or wot they call kicking up their 'eels. Cakes with pink icing and weak tea is about their speed."

148

I released my pent-up breath slowly and was conscious of a faintly perceptible easing of tension.

Uncle Joe turned back to Eileen and asked, "When did Uncle Jimmy tell you that story about the man who had his head almost cut off with a razor?"

He was between me and the door, and I put my clammy hands behind me to hide their shaking.

"Oh, that was long ago," Eileen piped, "only I remembered it when that happened to Uncle Jimmy. Somebody said his head was cut off too—and that's not true, is it, Uncle Joe?" Her round, earnest gaze fastened on him, full of childish trouble, and she looked to be on the verge of tears.

I made a movement, and Uncle Joe's eyes leaped to me for a moment before he said soothingly, "No, no, no—nothing like that. He'd been messed around and killed, but—nothing like that. You—is that what you told the policeman when he came here tonight and talked to you? Aunt Esther says a policeman came while we were out."

"Yes," the child said, "and he talked to me all alone, too, when I came here to go to bed. He asked me all sorts of things, and I told him about that man—right here in Kalgoorlie. It happened, didn't it, Uncle Joe?"

He looked at her, his eyelids heavy and his shoulders slumped, and after a moment she went on: "He said he wanted me to tell the other policeman all about it tomorrow. Do you think I shall have to go on the witness stand, Uncle Joe?"

"P'r'aps, little 'un—I dunno." He was silent for a space, and then he said, with something of his usual belligerence, "No! you're going to spend your Christmas in Perth. Only I won't be there, Eileen—I'll be somewhere where they can fix me 'ead. You see, I'm sick, lovey—I'm what they call a bit off me rocker."

He jerked his head around and gave me a long, level stare. "I'm mad, all right—ain't I, girl? Finish painting me own pictures and don't remember about it—and buy jujubes instead of pills for me 'ealth."

I nodded speechlessly, and Eileen began to whimper. He turned back to her and said caressingly, "Don't cry, lovey—there's a good girl. Everything's going to be all right, and you'll be one of the richest young nobs in town. I'll be in the asylum, and you can come and see your old uncle."

"But you're not off your head, Uncle Joe," Eileen protested, in tears.

"Yes, I am, lovey—yes, I am. Wait till I tell you what I've been doing. You can remember it all your life, and you'll know what I tell will be the truth—never mind about all the lies you'll hear."

Eileen said, "Yes, Uncle Joe," and he turned to me.

"Sit down girl, and listen—and stop shaking in your boots. I'm not going to 'urt you."

I sat down, silent and watchful, and he said firmly, "In the first place, that fellow here in Kalgoorlie that your Uncle Jimmy told you about was scum, so don't worry your head over him—he got what he deserved.

"As for your Grandfather George, he was too stingy with all that money, and he didn't enjoy life the way he was, so I thought I'd trip him up on the stairs and see what happened."

"Did you?" Eileen asked, absorbed.

"I did, little 'un. I put a toggle bolt in on the blank wall side and covered it over with wallpaper, and then I waited for a good opportunity to tie a piece of string from it across to the banisters. I fixed it up bright and early one morning, and old George went crashing and banging all the way to the bottom. I started to creep out of me room to cut the string away, so that nobody could find it—and that redheaded woman was there looking at me. I stopped with the scissors in me 'and and 'ad a good look at her face.

"Like a cat on hot bricks, she was. She says, 'Hurry, hurry, you fool,' and took the scissors and started cutting the string—and I went back into me room wondering what was up. I found out later that she thought the money would go straight to Wilfred if they had me up for George's murder. She left that same day, but she wrote me a letter saying she was me niece, Cleo Ballister, and since she was broke, I'd better brass up. I didn't send her much, but I told her to come and pay us a visit and I'd give her more. She agreed to come, after a while, just as we were setting off for Melbourne, so I arranged for her to come back with us, and we were to meet at the station. Well, when we got to the station, it wasn't the red-'aired 'ussy who met us, but this other one—this one sitting in the room with us 'ere."

He paused, while he and Eileen both regarded me gravely. I remained quiet under their combined gaze, and presently Uncle Joe shifted his heavy body and puffed through his walrus.

"I didn't know what was up, so I just let it go, and then, in Melbourne, the real Cleo turned up when we got on the train for Adelaide. Came to me bold as brass and said, 'Come clean, you old buzzard—what gives?'

"I ticked her off, though—told her to mind her manners and to tell me what was going on—because I didn't know. See, we couldn't understand why this Virginia Peters was taking Cleo's place, until Cleo heard something and found it was just an accident. The next thing I knew, Cleo had dyed her hair yellow and told me to keep my mouth shut, because she liked the situation. She was in love with some chap and didn't want Jimmy bothering her—told me to pay him off and get rid of him.

"She was in a bit of a wax about this bloke Butler, though—said she was sorry she'd missed out on that, but wot with her yellow hair and all, she could probably pick him up anyway.

"I'd been thinking that if I could only get the girl out of the way, everything would be rosy. Jimmy would think George's murderer was dead, because he really thought Cleo had done it.

"But she hadn't, lovey—I did it meself. All the care I took over that one, too—and that was the one that tripped me up. The other two went like a blooming breeze—no one the wiser. Ah well, they'll be 'ere after me any minute now. There's been one treading on me 'eels all night, and the others will soon be 'ere."

Eileen began to cry again, and he petted her until she was quiet.

"I've got to tell the rest, lovey. Now, I didn't like this new blonde, Cleo, much, but I put up with her until I had that attack of indigestion and lost me lizard. I'd sent Esther along to the diner to look for the creature, and I told your father, Wilfred, to go and take a walk, because his face was making me feel depressed. He got narked and went out, and the next minute that 'ussy Cleo came in. Said she'd decided she wanted a lump sum of money from me—a large sum—too much. She had a cheek, that one.

"I got out of my bunk and told her straight what I thought of her and where she could go. She never blinked an eye. Said all right, but she thought she'd go in and see Esther and tell her all about it. She went into Esther's compartment, too—I saw her—but I knew Es wasn't there. I was in a fine rage by that time, and I got me razor and went after her. She was sitting in the lower bunk, and I picked up Es's traveling clock and bashed her over the head. She was stunned, and I took me razor—"

Eileen gave a frightened cry, and I stood up and moved over to the bed.

Uncle Joe said, "Hush, lovey—it's all right. Sit down, girl. That one was bad in every way—she deserved it. I wiped me razor and pulled the bedclothes up over her. Her purse fell on the floor, and I picked it up and stuffed it in that 'orrid red 'oldall this one was using for a purse. Thought it might help her to clear the cobwebs out of her brain. Then I came back to me own compartment. There was no one in the corridor, and after I'd closed me door I washed the razor and put it away. I got into bed, and then Esther came back and said she was sorry she'd been so long, but she'd had a yarn with one of the waiters. Wilfred came back with her—I suppose 'e'd gorn after her to complain about the way I'd spoken to him.

"That's the way to do a murder, y'know—quick and brash, and no fiddling about the details. I took too much trouble over old George, and that's what did it for me. Jimmy saw me buy the toggle bolt, but I was always buying tools and things, and he didn't start thinking until I killed Cleo the same way I killed that scum here in Kalgoorlie. He put two and two together after that, but he didn't say anything. I wasn't frightened of Jimmy—he was frightened of me. I could see it in his face. Every time he looked at me he cringed—yellow, that boy was.

"I was beginning to realize that I'd have to get rid of him some-time, and then this afternoon I was in me compartment with the door open, and I saw him pass by with a paintbox in his hand. I went to the door to see what he was up to, and he sneaked along until he saw that the door to the compartment where I'd killed Cleo was open, so he went in.

"I thought it must be him who'd been mucking my paintings about, and I lost me temper and decided to do for him then and there.

"I took a paperweight and me razor and followed him, and I found him putting the paintbox into a suitcase. I bashed him over the head, and he fell on the bunk, so I cut his ruddy throat and then covered him with the sheet."

Eileen began to sob hysterically, and I stood up again, but Uncle Joe snarled at me, "Sit down, girl—and don't let me have to tell you again."

I perched warily on the edge of my chair, and he went on: "Yellow and all as that boy was, the bloody little swine had painted a toggle bolt in the hand of my aborigine—laying the foundation for blackmail, as I see it. I didn't notice it until too late, or I could have painted it out. But Wilfred was in with me, and I had to do something, so I slashed me masterpiece to ribbons and took care to cut the toggle bolt out and put it in me pocket.

"When I was talking to those reporters I pulled out me handker-chief, and out came that little bit of paper, and fell on the floor. Brewster was beside me, and 'e picked it up. 'Oh,' 'e says, 'this is part of your painting that you tore up, isn't it?' and walks off with it still in 'is 'and.

"I don't know 'ow long it'll take them—but some fine day they'll look into George's accident, and then they'll find that expansion shield behind the plaster and the hole I filled in when I took the bolt out. They'll know it's me then, because I tore up the picture and kept the part with the toggle bolt. After that they'll look up the old murder here in Kalgoorlie which some of them thought I'd done—and which I 'ad."

He laughed heartily and then stopped to listen to the unmistakable sounds of footsteps in the hall.

" 'Ere they come—the 'alf-witted dunces," he said cheerfully.

Chapter Thirty
THE BEAUTIES OF SALE

OLD JOHN, with a cup of tea balanced precariously in one hand, was peering through his glasses at a geranium.

"He's going to spill it in a minute," Clive observed.

"It doesn't matter at all," Clive's sister said composedly. "I serve tea in the garden to save the housework, anyway. Now, Virgineeah, tell me—what did happen in that railway carriage on your way to Albury?"

"I remember it quite clearly now," I replied. "We talked awhile, and I showed her the snapshot of me that Aunt Shep had sent. She liked it and asked if she might keep it—and she gave me one of herself in exchange. I put it in that pocket in the bottom of my suitcase—and Cleo later pasted it into my passport. We had the berths made up, and I went to bed. I had helped Cleo put the suitcases up in the top berth, because she said they were in her way and she needed room to put on her makeup. She went out to the lounge car, and it must have been quite late when she came back. I woke up to find her trying to pull the suitcases down so that she could get into the upper berth, and I said, 'Wait a minute, Cleo, I'll help you.' I remember getting out of bed and reaching up, and then the suitcases came down on top of us—and that's all."

Clive put his empty teacup onto the table and took out a cigarette. "So they took Cleo to the hospital—and gave her the wrong name, and she thought it was funny. Then she started wondering why Ginny hadn't got in touch with her—and when she caught up with Ginny of course she was profoundly puzzled, until she found out what had happened. Anything else, Effie?"

"Well"—Effie bit into a sandwich and squinted into the sunlight—"why did that man Joe go to the trouble of using a toggle bolt to hold the string when a tack or almost anything would have done?"

Clive shook his head. "That string had to be very taut, or it would have been seen, and he needed a bolt that would not loosen when he pulled the string around the banister. Since he was interested in tools and carpentry, he knew exactly what to use."

"Who finished the paintings and put the lollies in the wretched man's pillbox?" Effie asked after a moment.

"I'm quite sure that it was Aunt Esther," I said soberly. "I believe she thought that Uncle Joe wasn't quite right in the head anyway, and it galled her to see him spending that money right and left. She was afraid there wouldn't be any for Wilfred. She has never said anything, though, and Uncle Joe declares now that he did it himself—because he wants to be declared insane."

Effie nodded and asked, "Will you have more tea?" and Clive threw his cigarette away and turned on me.

"I intend to make every effort to like your friends, but something tells me that Marge is going to stick in my throat. She made a bad first impression."

I accepted more tea and a pink cake and quietly ground my teeth.

"If you ever mention that telegram again," I said firmly, "I'll howl like a dog. It was only a joke, anyway. Cleo had been telling us that Bill had arranged a man for her on the trip west. She didn't tell us about Jimmy, naturally, but said it was just to keep the men from bothering her. Marge said she was putting on side—whatever that means—and told me that if this Butler man had any money I ought to try and pick him up myself. We were all laughing, and none of it was serious."

"Cheek," said Clive, and began to wind one of my synthetic curls around his finger.

"Now wait a minute, you two," Effie interrupted. "I'm still not clear on the thing. Why did the girl come to Perth disguised in that outlandish fashion?"

"That was just typical Cleo," I explained. "I've remembered that part of it only recently, because she was very secretive about that trip. I was the only one who knew what she was doing—and she didn't break down and tell me until just before she left. She'd made some money on a horse and decided to make the trip and look up her relatives, who'd been urging her to come. I remember her saying, 'Uncle George is leaving all his money to Uncle Joe—and when Uncle Joe gets it he'll leave half to me and half to my cousin Wilfred. But that's too long to wait. I'm going to put on a false face and stay in Aunt Esther's boardinghouse—and that way I can see what personality is best to use on old George. I'm going to work on him to give me something now. I need it.'

"She was quite pleased with the idea—said it would give her a chance to use her acting ability—and Cleo always fancied herself as an actress.

But she was too impulsive, and it got the better of her. She caught Uncle Joe on the landing when he came out to cut the string—and she took the scissors out of his hand and cut the string herself, in order to cover him up. And Jimmy saw her. She left at once, after that, but she wrote to Uncle Joe and got some money out of him.

"I know she was scared for some months there—Jimmy writing her letters and Uncle Joe insisting that she come and pay them a visit. She was afraid to go—but after a while she nerved herself up to face it and she persuaded me to take the trip with her. I was only too happy. I'd wanted to make that trip ever since I landed in Sydney—but Old John wouldn't do it."

"What's that?" Old John asked vaguely, pottering back to us.

"I was saying that I'm afraid you'll have to come to Sale and live."

"Sale?" he repeated, blinking at me. "What's that?"

"It's a dot on the map—if the map makers remember to put it down at all. But it contains many beautiful and rare specimens."

"Where is it?"

"Victoria."

"No," said Old John. "I don't like Victoria—never did. Silly sort of place."

"That's rather snap judgment, when you've never even seen it, sir," Clive put in, looking annoyed.

Old John gave him an abstracted glance and said, "What do you want to go to a place like that for, Gin? We have our comfortable flat on Macquarrie Street, overlooking all those flowers in the Botanical Gardens. I doubt whether Jane would consent to go, anyway—she's particular—and my sister Jane's cooking is the only kind that I can eat."

"Sale," said Clive firmly, "has the most beautiful flowers in the world."

"What is it, Gin?" Old John asked unhappily. 'Why do you want to live in this fella's home town? Silly rabbit hutch of a place like that?"

"I have to. I want to drum up a few patients for him to work on—otherwise our six children might be undernourished."

THE END

Other Rue Morgue vintage mysteries

The Black Honeymoon
by Constance & Gwenyth Little

Can you murder someone with feathers? If you don't believe that feathers can kill, then you probably haven't read one of the 21 mysteries by the two Little sisters, the reigning queens of the cozy screwball mystery from the 1930s to the 1950s. No, Uncle Richard wasn't tickled to death—though we can't make the same guarantee for readers—but the hyperallergic rich man did manage to sneeze himself into the hereafter in his hospital room.

Suspicion falls on his nurse, young Miriel Mason, who recently married the dead man's nephew, Ian Ross, an army officer on furlough. Ian managed to sweep Miriel off her feet and to the altar—well, at least to city hall—before she had a chance to check his bank balance, which was nothing to boast about. In fact, Ian cheerfully explains that they'll have to honeymoon in the old family mansion and hope that his relations can leave the two lovebirds alone.

But when Miriel discovers that Ian's motive for marriage may have had nothing to do with her own charms, she decides to postpone at least one aspect of the honeymoon, installing herself and her groom in separate bedrooms. To clear herself of Richard's murder, Miriel summons private detective Kelly, an old crony of her father's, who gets himself hired as a servant in the house even though he can't cook, clean or serve. While Kelly snoops, the body count continues to mount at an alarming rate. Nor is Miriel's hapless father much help. Having squandered the family fortune, he now rents out rooms in his mansion and picks up a little extra cash doing Miriel's laundry.

Originally published in 1944, *The Black Honeymoon* is filled with tantalizing questions: Who is moaning in the attic. . .what is the terrible secret in the family Bible. . .why does Aunt Violet insist on staying in her room. . .will Kelly get fired for incompetence before he nabs the killer. . .will Miriel and Ian ever consummate their marriage? Combining the charm and laughs of a Frank Capra movie with the eccentric characters of a George S. Kaufmann play, *The Black Honeymoon* is a delight from start to finish. **0-915230-21-6**   **$14**

The Black Gloves
by Constance & Gwenyth Little

"I'm relishing every madcap moment."—*Murder Most Cozy*

Welcome to the Vickers estate near East Orange, New Jersey, where the middle class is destroying the neighborhood, erecting their horrid little cottages, playing on the Vickers tennis court, and generally disrupting the comfortable life of Hammond Vickers no end.

It's bad enough that he had to shell out good money to get his daughter Lissa a divorce in Reno only to have her brute of an ex-husband show up on his doorstep. But why does there also have to be a corpse in the cellar? And lights going on and off in the attic?

Lissa, on the other hand, welcomes the newcomers into the neighborhood, having spotted a likely candidate for a summer beau among them. But when she hears coal being shoveled in the cellar and finds a blue dandelion near a corpse, what's a girl gonna do but turn detective, popping into people's cottages and dipping dandelions into their inkwells looking for a color match. And she'd better catch the killer fast, because Detective Sergeant Timothy Frobisher says that only a few nail files are standing between her and jail.

Originally published in 1939, *The Black Gloves* was one of 21 wacky mysteries written by the Little sisters and is a sparkling example of the light-hearted cozy mystery that flourished between the Depression and the Korean War. It won't take you long to understand why these long out-of-print titles have so many ardent fans.   **0-915230-20-8 $14**

The Rue Morgue Press intends to eventually publish all 21 of the Little mysteries.

Murder is a Collector's Item
by Elizabeth Dean

"Completely enjoyable"—*New York Times*. "Fast and funny."—*The New Yorker*.

Twenty-six-year-old Emma Marsh isn't much at spelling or geography and perhaps she butchers the odd literary quotation or two, but she's a keen judge of character and more than able to hold her own when it comes to selling antiques or solving murders. When she stumbles upon the body of a rich collector on the floor of the Boston antiques shop where she works, suspicion quickly falls upon her missing boss. Emma knows Jeff Graham is no murderer, but veteran homicide cop Jerry Donovan doesn't share her conviction.

With a little help from Hank Fairbanks, her wealthy boyfriend and would-be criminologist, Emma turns sleuth and cracks the case, but not before a host of cops, reporters and customers drift through the shop on Charles Street, trading insults and sipping scotch as they talk clues, prompting a *New York Times* reviewer to remark that Emma "drinks far more than a nice girl should."

Emma does a lot of things that women didn't do in detective novels of the 1930s. In an age of menopausal spinsters, deadly sirens, admiring wives and air-headed girlfriends, pretty, big-footed Emma Marsh stands out. She's a precursor of the independent women sleuths that finally came into their own in the last two decades of this century.

Originally published in 1939, *Murder is a Collector's Item* was the first of three books featuring Emma. Smoothly written and sparkling with dry, sophisticated humor, it combines an intriguing puzzle with an entertaining portrait of a self-possessed young woman on her own in Boston toward the end of the Great Depression. Author Dean, who worked in a Boston antiques shop, offers up an insider's view of what that easily impressed *Times* reviewer called the "goofy" world of antiques. Lovejoy, the rogue antiques dealer in Jonathan Gash's mysteries, would have loved Emma.   **0-915230-19-4 $14**

Murder, Chop Chop
by James Norman

"The book has the butter-wouldn't-melt-in-his-mouth cool of Rick in *Casablanca.*" —*The Rocky Mountain News.* "Amuses the reader no end."— *Mystery News.* "This long out-of-print masterpiece is intricately plotted, full of eccentric characters and very humorous indeed. Highly recommended."—*Mysteries by Mail*

You'll find a cipher or two to crack, a train with a mind of its own, and Chiang Kai-shek's false teeth to cloud the waters in this 1942 classic tale of detection and adventure set during the Sino-Japanese war, with the sleuthing honors going to a gigantic Mexican guerrilla fighter named Gimiendo Quinto and a beautiful Eurasian known as Mountain of Virtue.   **0-915230-16-X $13**

Cook Up a Crime
by Charlotte Murray Russell

"Some wonderful old-time recipes...highly recommended."—*Mysteries by Mail.*

Meet Jane Amanda Edwards, a self-styled "full-fashioned" spinster who complains she hasn't looked at herself in a full-length mirror since Helen Hokinson started drawing for *The New Yorker.* But you can always count on Jane to look into other people's affairs, especially when there's a juicy murder case to investigate. In this 1951 title Jane goes looking for recipes (included between chapters) and finds a body instead. As usual, in one of the longest running jokes in detective fiction, her lily-of-the-field brother Arthur is found clutching the murder weapon.   **0-915230-18-6 $13**

The Man from Tibet
by Clyde B. Clason

"The novels of American classicist Clason have been unavailable for years, a lapse happily remedied with the handsome trade paperback reprint of (Westborough's)best known case. Clason spun ornate puzzles in the manner of Carr and Queen and spread erudition as determinedly as Van Dine."—Jon L. Breen, *Ellery Queen's Mystery Magazine.* "A highly original and practical locked-room murder method."— Robert C.S. Adey.

The elderly historian, Prof. Theocritus Lucius Westborough, solves a cozy 1938 locked room mystery involving a Tibetan lama in Chicago in which the murder weapon may well be an eighth century manuscript. A fair-play puzzler for fans of John Dickson Carr. With an extensive bibliography, it is also one of the first popular novels to examine in depth forbidden Tibet and Tibetan Buddhism.   **0-915230-17-8 $14**

As part of its vintage mystery series, The Rue Morgue Press intends to publish more titles by many of the authors appearing in this catalog as well as books by Manning Coles (the four ghost books), Joanna Cannan, Glyn Carr and other important writers whose books have been unavailable for many years.

Our only non-vintage reprint is one of the most popular novels in recent years

The Mirror
by Marlys Millhiser

"Completely enjoyable."—*Library Journal* "A great deal of fun."—*Publishers Weekly.*

How could you not be intrigued, as one reviewer pointed out, by a novel in which "you find the main character marrying her own grandfather and giving birth to her own mother?" Such is the situation in Marlys Millhiser's classic novel (a Mystery Guild selection originally published by Putnam in 1978) of two women who end up living each other's lives after they look into an antique Chinese mirror.

Twenty-year-old Shay Garrett is not aware that she's pregnant and is having second thoughts about marrying Marek Weir when she's suddenly transported back 78 years in time into the body of Brandy McCabe, her own grandmother, who is unwillingly about to be married off to miner Corbin Strock. Shay's in shock but she still recognizes that the picture of her grandfather that hangs in the family home doesn't resemble her husband-to-be. But marry Corbin she does and off she goes to the high mining town of Nederland, where this thoroughly modern young woman has to learn to cope with such things as wood cooking stoves and—to her—old-fashioned attitudes about sex. Shay's ability to see into the future has her mother-in-law thinking she's a witch and others calling her a psychic but Shay was an indifferent student at best and not all of her predictions hit the mark: remember that "day of infamy" when the Japanese attacked Pearl Harbor—Dec. *11*, 1941?

In the meantime, Brandy McCabe is finding it even harder to cope with life in the Boulder, Colorado of 1978. After all, her wedding is about to be postponed due to her own death—at least the death of her former body—at the age of 98. And, in spite of the fact she's a virgin, she's about to give birth. And *this* young woman does have some very old-fashioned ideas about sex, which leaves her husband-to-be—and father of her child—very puzzled. *The Mirror* is even more of a treat for today's readers, given that it is now a double trip back in time. Not only can readers look back on life at the turn of the century, they can also revisit the days of disco and the sexual revolution of the 1970's.

So how does one categorize *The Mirror?* Is it science fiction? Fantasy? Supernatural? Mystery? Romance? Historical fiction? You'll find elements of each but in the end it's a book driven by that most magical of all literary devices. imagine if   0-915230-15-1 $14.95

For more information on Rue Morgue Press titles write

The Rue Morgue Press
POBox 4119
Boulder, CO 80306